K.R JONES

Possessions

Book One in the MSMI Series

www.facebook.com/KRJonesOfficial

First edition

This book was professionally typeset on Reedsy.
Find out more at reedsy.com

Acknowledgement

Dedicated to my Mum and Dad for never giving up on me, and believing in my dreams

ABBREVIATIONS

NCLB UK – NATIONAL CRIMINAL LAW BUREAU UNITED KINGDOM

MSMI – MANSLAUGHTER AND MURDER INVESTIGATION (AGENTS)

CS – CRIME SCENE

M – MURDER

ABH – ACTUAL BODILY HARM

GBH – GRIEVOUS BODILY HARM

PWITS – POSSESSION WITH INTENTION TO SUPPLY (ILLEGAL DRUGS)

NHMW –– NICK HARDY AND MARTHA WILLIS UNIT NAME

CSI – Crime Scene Investigators

BSU – Burglary Specialist Unit

ME – Medical Examiner

CHAPTER ONE

Detective Martha Willis stood in the open doorway, taken aback by the horrific scene laid out before her. The cabin was old and run down, and debris of broken glass and rotted furniture lay scattered about. The rotting wooden floor was speckled with dried blood, emphasising the horror that had taken place.

Edging further into what was once the "living room", her view of the mutilated corpse became clearer. Martha felt a sudden rush of guilt, unable to maintain her professional demeanour. Within minutes her mind became overwhelmed with that guilt, and it was not long before she found herself being consumed by a dark cloud, finally succumbing to the sweet embrace of oblivion.

* * *

Another day in the office, paperwork still covering most of my desk. I wonder how long I can make my next break last? Martha thought. She had been in the office since 6:30 am and found that time was dragging. It already felt as though she had been in situ for the whole day, but it was only 8:40 am. Just over 2 hours. Come on, come on! Lunchtime couldn't come quick enough.

"Martha?" Fellow Detective, Nick Hardy, walked through the open door. He was holding a folder with UK NCLB: *MSMI Department, #3796, CS – M.* (UK National Criminal Law Bureau: Manslaughter and Murder Investigation Department, folder #3796, Crime Scene – Murder) printed on the front.

Great.

"Yes, Nick?" Martha replied, clearly agitated by the presence of the folder.

"We have a case," Detective Nick Hardy made his way to Martha's desk. "A call just came in. A young woman found dead and beaten in a back alley. We're needed at the scene."

Grabbing her coat, Martha made her way out of the office, Nick following close beside her. *It's going to be a long day,* she thought.

* * *

Arriving in Nick's black unmarked Mazda CX-3, Martha prepared herself mentally for the scene to come. After working on many cases and always remaining one of the best at her job, she still found herself getting nervous and queasy when facing a murder scene up close.

The wind was bitterly cold as Martha and Nick exited the car, the blast of frigid cold air prompting Martha to place her hands into her coat pockets. Making their way down the no-named back alley in Whitechapel East London, just off the Commercial Road, the smell of death slowly reached her nose. Police tape was spread across the alley to keep unwanted pedestrians from entering the crime scene. It was a narrow, quiet place, still awaiting the renovations the area was undergoing to bring it back into use. Discoloured bricks and broken windows made up a large disused building on one side, on the other a more modern-looking building with barred windows, also disused, towered up, enclosing the area completely. The ground was an old and broken cobblestone walkway, many of the cobbles missing, leaving holes and an uneven surface to trip up the unwary.

Great day to have chosen heels. Flats in future, Martha thought. She made her way under the tape with Nick, ID at the ready to gain access to the scene.

"I'm Detective Martha Willis and this is my partner, Detective Nick Hardy." She held her ID at a short distance from a uniformed officer's face and was given immediate access. They made their way over to the small forensic tent which covered the body, protecting any possible evidence and hiding the corpse from prying eyes. Forensics was already busy taking notes and photographing the body and the surrounding area, examining what they could on the scene. Once satisfied that they had gleaned all possible information on site, they would give the thumbs up to transporting the body back for a full post-mortem.

The dead woman's eyes had been pale blue and emotionless, already clouded over with the mist of death. Her strawberry blonde coloured hair was thickly clotted with blood and dirt. She looked so young, perhaps early 20s? Her lips were cut and bruises covered her naked body, indicating she had faced a brutal beating before having her life cruelly taken away. Her legs appeared as though they had been forced apart, and as a result, had been broken near the top, her hip bone looking as though it was severely damaged.

Poor girl.

"Hello, I am Jessica Heath," a woman of around 30 approached the two detectives and held out her hand to Martha in greeting. They shook. "I am a Forensic Anthropologist," she said in a clipped, precise manner.

"Nice to meet you. I'm Detective Willis. Can we confirm an age for the victim? And have any clothes been found belonging to this young woman?"

"From her appearance, we can only estimate her age between eighteen to late twenties, we can give a more accurate age once a full autopsy is held. No clothes have been found anywhere near the crime scene, so no paper ID, such as a driver's license, to tell us who she is. We are searching for any evidence that might tell us if she was wearing clothes when she arrived here, but as of yet we have not found any."

"The bruises and cuts?"

"The bruises appear to be consistent with that of a severe beating and being forcibly restrained. There also appears to be wounds on both of her hands that are consistent with the victim attempting to defend herself. I believe, under the circumstances, that we can safely deduce that the bruising took place whilst she was still alive. A quick examination indicates that the cuts were probably caused by a blunt weapon. With the volume of blood present and the placing of the body, we can confirm that this is where our victim died."

"Was she," she didn't want to bring herself to say the next word. She forced it. "Was she raped?"

"We cannot give a definitive report on what happened until we have carried out a post-mortem. Until then, we can logically assume that a sexual attack *may* have taken place due to the breaks in her ischium and the excessive bruising around her wrists and both thighs. Particulates found in the flesh wounds on her wrists seem to indicate she was tied up with rope at some point. The ligature markings around her cheeks and behind both ears suggest she was gagged by some kind of rough cloth. Also, it looks as though she suffered multiple amounts of sexual abuse. Until a full autopsy has taken place, I am afraid I cannot help much for now and can only give educated guesses."

"Thank you, Miss Heath." Martha made her way over to Nick who had gone over to interview the woman who found the victim.

"I was just, I was walking home from work and she was just, laying there! I just . . ." she broke down into tears, renewing the trail of dried tears with new ones.

"Thank you for your co-operation. If we've any more questions to ask we will let you know." Nick walked off to the side with Martha, notebook in hand. "Her name is Leanne Baker. She doesn't know much; just found the body by accident. I doubt she'll be sleeping any time soon. She works night shifts, left for home about 6 this morning. She called the police the moment she found the body at around 6:45."

"We don't have an ID for the victim, and her clothes have yet to be found," Martha informed him.

"Forensics and Missing Persons may help us find the answer to that. Anything else?" He folded his notebook away into his coat pocket and blew on his hands, rubbing them together to try and get some warmth back into them.

"Forensics won't confirm anything as fact until they've run a full autopsy. With no clothes on the scene and the state of the body, they will only assume this to be a possible rape and murder victim."

"And no witnesses by the looks of things. Unless we catch a break with DNA this could be a long one."

The interviews, examinations and photography continued until around 14:30. The afternoon was much colder than before, and after 5 hours on the scene everything was eventually packed up and taken away for further investigation. Martha slid lazily into Nick's car, hunger written across her face, with her stomach doing summersaults. *Okay, okay, I'll feed you!*

"Burger King?" Nick asked as though he had read Martha's mind. She smiled in agreement, easing herself into a comfortable position for the half-hour journey back.

CHAPTER TWO

The late Burger King lunch was just what the Doctor ordered. 17:27. Martha and Nick sat in their office together, finishing writing up their report from the murder scene to add to the Case Folder.

"I believe that's the last of the paperwork for today." Martha yawned, placing a few sheets of paper into the folder. "It's sad. Cases like this make me wonder what the fuck is going on in the sicko's head!"

"I know. We'll catch the bastard though. Hopefully, it won't be too long until we get an ID on the victim"

"Oh," Martha placed her head in both hands. "When we get it, we'll have to trace her family and let them know. Sometimes I wonder why I chose this profession."

"It's okay. We'll do it together." He placed a hand on her arm and rubbed gently to lend some comfort. "Come on, I'll drop you off at home."

The ride home left Martha feeling very grateful. *Anything beats a bus home in the middle of London.* She ran herself a hot bath, hoping for a relaxing escape from the long day she'd had. She lay back and was left with just her thoughts. *That poor woman. So young, her life brutally taken away. What must have been racing through her mind during the attack? Pain, fear, sickness. Such a horrible thing to fall victim to.*

The phone began to ring. She forced herself out of the bath with great agitation. *Some alone time wouldn't go amiss, you know!*

"Hello?" She asked coldly.

"Hey Martha, it's me, Tyler." An old friend. Been almost a month since their last conversation. *What does she want?*

"Hi. You okay?"

"Yeah, I'm just calling to see if you'd like to go out for dinner?" *Why now? I'm tired, drained and just want some rest*, she thought.

"Could we do it some other time? I'd love to catch up, but it has been a very long day."

"Yeah 'course. You alright though? Nothing's happened, has it?"

"I'm fine. Everything is fine." Impatient. *Please, give me some peace already. Try again tomorrow.*

"Alright. Speak soon." The phone hung up.

Peace. She changed into her pyjamas and made herself a hot chocolate, laid up in bed and finished the day with gratitude for the night.

* * *

6:30 am. The phone was ringing for the third attempt on reaching Martha, who reluctantly forced herself from her bed.

"Yeah?" Groggy.

"Hey Martha, it's me, Nick. We're going to need you in early today, is that alright?

Not really, I'm tired.

"Yeah, sure thing."

"I'll be round in 10." The phone hung up.

Martha went to the bathroom to splash her face with cold water. *Wakey wakey.* She rushed around her apartment to ready herself for another

7

day's work. She was slipping on her second shoe when she received a text message.

I'm here. C u in a sec.
Nick.

She rushed out of the apartment and made her way to Nick's Mazda. It was dark and brutally cold out, like sharp miniature teeth sinking into her cheeks. Misty rain fell gracefully as she opened the door to the CX-3 and sank into the passenger seat.

"I bought you a hot chocolate," Nick passed the drink over. *Such a lovely gesture.*

"Thanks." Nick started the engine and they sat in silence for a few minutes. "So, what's the reason behind this early morning?"

"We believe we have identified the victim from missing persons." He reached down into the pocket of his door while keeping his eyes on the road, pulling out and passing over a folder.

Martha opened the folder to see the picture of a beautiful blonde-haired girl who looked exactly like the victim from the alley. "Certainly looks like her, minus cuts and bruising." She flicked through the paperwork.

"Lisa Marsh. Dental procedures have taken place as part of the autopsy. I'm just waiting on a message confirming if they're a match or not."

"And where are we going at this ungodly hour?"

"To this young lady's home," indicating the folder on Martha's lap, "where her mum lives. It's about an hour away. We'll have the dental records by then."

"And you're sure it'll be a match?"

"One hundred per cent sure. Minus the bruises and cuts to her face, as you say, there is no doubt that it's her." Martha began to talk but

Nick interrupted quickly. "And before you say it, there are no records of her having a twin."

Well, that shut me up. Nick's phone bleeped.

"Could you check that for me?" He pulled his mobile from his pocket and handed it over to Martha.

"It's David Mace from the DNA Analysis and Research lab. He's confirming that the dental records are a match with our victim's. She's our girl alright." An 'I-told-you-so' smile crept across Nick's face as he gave Martha a sneaky wink. Martha rolled her eyes mockingly. *Men.*

She continued looking through the file, looking at the life this young lady had once led.

Name: Lisa Marsh.

Sex: Female.

DOB: 12/06/1992

Age: 24 Years, 7 Months.

Race: White.

Height: 5'4".

Hair: Blonde.

Eyes: Blue.

Last seen by: Mother, saying goodbye at the front door. Lisa left for work at their local Aldi. Never arrived at her workplace. Father deceased.

Poor girl. So young with her life before her, brutally taken away. She closed the file and stared out from the window. The sun was slowly beginning to rise as they arrived at Lisa's mum's house.

"How are we going to do this?" Nick asked, straight to the point as usual.

"I'll tell her." *I don't want to be the bearer of such horrific news, but it'll come better from me.*

"You sure?"

Not really. "Yes."

They got out of the car and made their way up to a small bungalow, its front garden looking a little overgrown and run down. Nick rang the doorbell. It didn't take long for a woman of around 50 to answer the door.

"Yes?" She asked warily, still dressed in her nightie.

"Hello. I'm Detective Willis and this is my partner Detective Hardy."

"What do you want?"

"We're here about your daughter, Lisa Marsh? We believe you reported her missing?"

"Yes. I did. Have you found her? Is she safe? Is she okay?" Hope rose in the woman's voice and Martha and Nick shared a sad look. "What? What is it? She is okay, isn't she?" The questions came in quick, short bursts.

"Can we come in, Miss Marsh?"

The lady let them in, concern written across her face. They sat together in a small living room, floral patterns being the theme of this woman's home. She offered the Detectives some tea which they politely declined. *It's time.*

"Miss Marsh," Martha began. "Yesterday morning a young lady was found in an alleyway."

"My Lisa?"

"Unfortunately, the woman was found deceased." Silence rang through the living room, Miss Marsh staring, unblinking at the Detectives. Martha cleared her throat and continued in a very soft voice. "Our Forensic team worked late last night and again early this morning, as no ID could be found for the victim. We're sorry to say-"

"No. No, it's not her!" Tears fell from her eyes, her face crumpled as it filled with disbelief and pain.

"I'm sorry. Dental records confirm that this woman was Lisa Marsh.

We're so sorry."

"But, it can't! She's my baby! My baby girl!" Her voice broke under the strain of pure heartbreak. 24 or 4, Lisa would always be this woman's little girl. "She was my life! How can I live without my baby? I should have protected her!"

"Miss Marsh, I completely understand the pain you must be feeling right now, but there was nothing anyone could have done." Martha began to feel herself filling up with tears.

"It was my job to protect her!" Anger, as well as sadness and grief, fought for dominance within her.

"Miss Marsh," Nick began to take over, seeing Martha's struggle of keeping back the tears. "We're so sorry to be bringing this news back to you, and I can only regret the news wasn't what we had all wished for. But there is absolutely no reason for you to blame yourself. You did everything you could, and even reported her missing which allowed us to know a young woman needed our help. Unfortunately, we didn't find her in time, but our job will not stop here. We promise you that we will find out what happened to Lisa, and that anyone involved in her death will be found and punished! I understand you are hurting, but right now we need you to stay strong to help us find the person who hurt your daughter. Do you think you can do that for us?"

Her tears began to subside, although the sadness was still present. Martha gave Nick a thankful smile, wiping away one stray tear and taking up her professional stance once again. *Okay, stay strong. This woman needs us, so I can't go losing control now!*

"Thank you," Martha said to her partner. Nick gave her a reassuring smile. *What would I do without him?* "We just need to ask a few questions that may help in solving this case, is that okay?"

"Yes. Yes of course." She rubbed a crumpled up tissue under her eyes to dry her tears.

"What route did Lisa usually take to work?"

"She walked. It's only a straight road. About fifteen minutes from here? Aldi, at the top of the street."

"But she never turned up?" Nick asked, making sure of the facts and writing down notes in the pad he had pulled from his blazer pocket.

"No. Her manager called. His name is Mark. He asked if she was ill but I told him she left for work about two hours beforehand. That's when I knew something was wrong. She never missed a day of work unless she was too ill to leave her bed. She is . . . was, so lovely and kind, and one of the most reliable people you could ever meet." She took a deep, steadying breath.

"Did she ever make trips into London? Central London?" Martha asked with curiosity building. *Something isn't quite right.*

"No. Not that I know of. I believe all of her friends live nearby. I've never known her to go to London, not even for shopping trips. Why? Is this important?" She looked confused.

"Well, it's just the alley she was found in was in London. When was it she went missing?"

"Two weeks ago, today."

"Monday the 9th of January?" *There's something.*

"Yes. And I reported her missing immediately after that, but due to her age they wouldn't record her as missing until 48 hours after the initial report, just in case she was out on her own free will without letting me know."

"Yes, of course. Did she have a boyfriend?"

"I'm not sure. There was one young lad she spent her free time with. I believe his name is Jason."

"Do you know his last name? Or where we can find him?"

"I think it was Stark. Jason Stark, yes. I'm not sure where he lives, though. I don't remember much about him. I'm sorry I can't be of much help."

"You're doing brilliantly, Miss Marsh. I'm sure we can find him from the name you have given."

"I reported my girl missing two weeks ago. Has my baby been dead this whole time?" Her voice grew shaky again. *I wish I knew,* thought Martha. *Definitely something.*

"We cannot confirm anything until we receive a report from our forensic team. They're working very hard, and we promise we will find out what happened to your daughter". Nick said.

They comforted Miss Marsh a bit longer, ensuring she was okay, before leaving the house and beginning their hour-long journey back to London. 9:10 am. The car was warm and cosy compared to the brittle bite of the wind outside. There was sure to be traffic on the way back.

"You seemed like you were onto something back there," Nick broke the silence.

"Did I? I was just, asking, you know?" *Real subtle.*

"Come on, Martha. We've known each other for years. I know when you know something and I know when you're lying. We're working this case together, so, out with it."

"It might be nothing. I was just thinking of what we know about the current state of the victim's body."

"And that is?"

"Well, her daughter was reported missing two weeks ago. She must have been alive up until recently."

"How do you mean?"

"Well, if a body is exposed to all elements; air, sunlight, water, whatever you can think of, we know that the decomposition process will happen very fast. It will also attract insects rather quickly which will accelerate the decomposition. Now, I'm no Forensic Scientist but.."

"But the body hadn't reached those stages of decomposition." Nick continued the sentence. *He's on the same page, good.* "So this means?"

"It could mean that she was still alive up to a couple of days ago. As I said, I'm not a forensic scientist so I can't say when she was killed exactly, Jessica will have the answer to that. But to me, the victim looked pretty normal, given the attack wounds. So depending on the state of her organs, she may not have been dead for more than a day or two."

"Fucking hell!"

Silence consumed the interior of the car once again as they let the conversation sink in.

"If this is the case, and it bloody well looks like it is," Nick broke the silence again. "Then that means she could have been doing numerous things in numerous places for two weeks."

Red lights. Nick stopped the car and put on the handbrake.

"She could have been out, wanting a bit of freedom from her mum who looks to be a little over-protective, partying in numerous clubs locally and further out like London, spending the nights with anyone who lived close enough, friends, guys she met at bars. Or . . ."

He paused.

"Or?" Martha pushed him on.

"Or she was taken at the beginning of the two weeks by some twisted fucker on her way to work. She could have been abducted and abused and hidden away for two weeks until the bastard killed her. All the while we had the chance to save her but didn't!" He grew agitated.

"Don't start blaming yourself. Like you said it could be any number of things."

A car horn beeped loudly from behind. The lights had changed to green. Handbrake off, drive on. Nick was still clearly agitated by the possibilities surrounding Lisa's disappearance.

"Look, if she was taken at the beginning of the two weeks and was hidden, that's neither your's nor anybody else's fault that she wasn't found in time. If she was hidden away then she could have been hidden anywhere. Just don't start kicking yourself over something that wasn't your fault. It was someone else's job to find her, and as you know most missing persons either never get found, or turn up dead when they do.

And when they do turn up dead, we take over. It's our job to find out what happened to her and find the prick that did this so we stop it from happening again. Okay?" The thought of a possible rapist and murderer on the loose stabbed at Martha's gut and encouraged her more to find the one behind Lisa's horrific attack.

"Thanks." Nick sighed, releasing the inner guilt in a puff of carbon dioxide.

No problem. Anything for you.

They travelled the rest of the journey back to the office in comfortable silence, each deep in their own, private thoughts. The traffic was minimal and they made it back to the station at 10:30 am.

CHAPTER THREE

One week after Lisa Marsh's body was found, Martha and Nick still had no leads on the killer. They both sat in their office, the heating set high to help them keep warm. The snow had hit hard during the week, causing temperatures to drop below zero.

"Excuse me?" A knock at the office door. Jessica stood there with an Autopsy Report folder in her hands. "We have finished our report and have determined the cause of death as well as other factors. I thought it would be easier to talk you through them?"

"Yes. Please, take a seat." Martha invited her in, eager to hear the results. Nick rose from his desk and joined Martha at hers, resting his butt on the edge whilst Jessica took the chair in front of them.

"What would you like me to start with?"

"I believe if you could tell it in the order it probably took place it could help us to see more clearly what happened?" Nick took out his notebook, preparing to write down the new findings.

"Yes, of course. I shall try my best." Her voice was soft and her diction was very clear. *This is it. Stay calm!* "Lisa Marsh, Female, 24 years of age. From the external examination, it is clear that she was a victim of a highly aggressive assault that involved both fists and a blunt weapon. She had defensive wounds on her palms which shows that she tried fighting off her attacker. She has one very deep cut on the centre of her left palm which is consistent with grabbing a blunt weapon, as though she attempted to pull it from the attacker's hand. The cut marks seem to match those of a small blunt kitchen knife, which unfortunately does not narrow it down for your search for a weapon. Kitchen knives are rather numerous. I am sorry."

"It's okay. Please, continue." Nick replied, keeping up with the newly found information.

"A few of the cuts and bruises around Lisa's body are estimated to be a couple of hours older than some of the attack wounds, such as the cut in her hand. It was quite deep so she lost a lot of blood through this period and caught an infection as a result, but from the examination, we can guess that the attacker tried stopping the blood flow by wrapping rags around it.

"We can also confirm that she had suffered from multiple broken ribs. Her left wrist was also broken as well as severe dislocation around her ischium. Internal examination shows that sperm was present around and in her pubic area."

Martha's breath caught in her lungs, failing to exhale. *No! Please, no!* A burning sensation in her throat grew. "She was . . ."

"Raped. Yes, I am sorry." Jessica seemed relatively calm compared to the fast-paced breathing that Martha was experiencing.

Nick walked around the desk to join her and wrapped an arm over her shoulder. "Hey, it's okay. Keep calm. I know it's hard, but I promise you I'm here."

"Would you like me to leave?"

"No. No, stay." Martha breathed out heavily. "We need to know. Please, I'm sorry." She regained control of herself and Nick pulled up a chair beside her. *Keep it together.*

"We found obscure lacerations in her vagina which is the result of rape, becoming less visible due to how long it was since the attack, and our autopsy taking place. We have taken semen specimens as well as pubic hair samples from the victim. This will hopefully help to ID the attacker when questioning and taking DNA samples of your suspects."

"Thank you," Nick said.

"How did she die?" Martha's voice was shaky.

"We found a bleed on the brain which also suffered raised intracranial pressure."

"Which means?" Both Martha and Nick together.

"This gives us two things. She has several fractures to the back of her skull which has caused some of the bone to be pushed inwards, piercing her brain and causing the bleed. This is consistent with receiving very hard, repeated blows to the back of the head. Looking at the impact marks on the skull, it looks as though her head was hit multiple times against a hard flat surface, like concrete flooring, which coincides with where and how she was found."

"The ground in the alley." Martha interrupted.

"Yes. It is consistent with having one's head hit against the ground with extreme force, and the marks appear to match the cobblestone flooring in the alley."

"And the pressure thing?" Nick pushed.

"The raised intracranial pressure can be caused by a few things, one of which is a brain tumour. This was then confirmed when we found an intracranial neoplasm. After running a few tests we found that this was a cancerous tumour. We can only estimate roughly by the size and severity of the tumour how long she may have lived if she had never been attacked and killed."

"How long?"

"Martha, I don't think that's something you need to hear." Nick tried reasoning with Martha, but deep down she felt this bubble of anger growing inside.

"Tell me, how long?" She pushed for more information.

"We can only predict that she would have maybe lived around five more years, give or take, depending on a diagnosis and treatment."

Martha just stared, somewhat incapable of taking this in.

"We can confirm her time of death due to the stage of decomposition in her organs. They were still in a reasonably healthy condition which tells us she was found between twenty-four and seventy-two hours after death."

"So she died just under two weeks after going missing?" Nick was the only one capable of communication with Jessica.

"Yes. Some marks are older than others, but only by a couple of days. We can assume that she was held against her will with someone she may or may not have known for around 3 days, the days she was missing before that we cannot account for. We can assume one likelihood of what took place is that from where she was held hostage, it may be possible that she tried escaping but was then caught by her attacker in the alley where she then suffered a beating which involved a blow to her head and rape. Whether the death was intentional or not, I cannot say."

"That son of a bitch!!" Martha's anger finally forced its way out, a thick black cloud of bitterness thrashing around her mind. *Sick bastard!*

"Thank you, Jessica. That was very helpful. If we have any more questions we'll call."

"No problem, Detective Hardy. I shall leave the autopsy report with you." She placed the folder on the desk and left the office quietly.

"Martha, it's okay. We've dealt with murder cases before. We'll catch him."

"It's not just murder though, is it? She was raped! She had limited time left in her life due to a tumour she probably didn't even know she had! The last moments of her life should have been filled with happiness; instead, she was tortured by some dickhead!"

"Martha, I understand that you are angry and so am I. But we have to be professional about this! If you're incapable of proceeding with this case suitably and calmly, then I'm sorry but we'll have to take you off."

"No! You can't take me off!" The anger she felt sank into sadness. *I can't be taken from this case. The victim needs me.*

"Why not? You know how we're meant to act, no matter how harsh the cases are. I don't want to have to take you off the case but if you can't handle it then I don't really have a choice, and you know that."

He has a point.

"I'm sorry. It's just hard. How she spent the last few days of her life, terrified and away from home. It's difficult to imagine all the emotions that she must have experienced."

"I know, I know," he placed his hand gently on Martha's knee, rubbing with his thumb in an attempt to reassure her. "I think you should take the rest of the day off. Have a soak in the bath and relax. Just, remember to keep yourself calm. We will catch this son of a bitch, whatever it takes. We have his DNA so it won't take us long to fuck up this rapist scum! I'll drive you home, and my phone will be by my side so you can contact me whenever you need to."

"Thank you, Nick." *Why must you be so caring and sweet?*

"It's no problem, honestly."

"No really, thank you so much." *I don't know what I'd do without you.*

His smile was warm and made Martha feel calmer. *Home it is. I need a break.*

CHAPTER FOUR

T he low groaning of the fridge hummed loudly around the apartment, the noise shortly interrupted by the slam of the front door. Martha took off her oversized black winter coat along with her gloves, scarf and woolly hat, hanging them all to the side. She switched the hall and living room lights on and decided the heating fireplace was a grand idea. 2:43 pm. *I've got the rest of the day to unwind. Relax.* Martha walked slowly into the kitchen and began microwaving tinned soup and readying some buttered bread for a late lunch. She reached out to open the fridge door when she noticed a sticky note staring back at her. *Okay. Weird. I didn't put that there.* She took it from the door and sat at the kitchen counter to read it.

It's my turn to
torture you!

The words stared at her and her breathing became shallow. The hairs on the back of her neck stood on end as a breeze ran over her body. She turned in an instant, looking around her empty apartment. *Someone has been in my home! Someone left me this note!*

BING!

"Shit!" Her heart skipped a beat as the microwave scared her back to reality. She ran straight for the house phone and begun to dial, but the phone was unresponsive. *What?* She followed the lead to ensure it was plugged in and switched on, only to find the wire had been cut clean in half. Her body began to shake with fear and panic. Her bedroom door slammed, bringing her body to attention and causing her heart to race.

"Who's there?" Silence. "What the fuck do you want with me?"

She made her way over to her bedroom slowly, her palms layered in sweat. She brought her right hand up to the door handle and took a deep breath.

1 . . .

2 . . .

3 . . .

She pulled the handle down fast and threw open the door. The window to her right was cracked open with the net curtain blowing lightly in the cold breeze. The room was otherwise empty. *Who the fuck got into my home and how?* Martha rushed over to the window, buzzing on adrenaline she slammed it shut and double-checked that she had locked it. Triple checked. She ran back to her coat on the hook near the front door and pulled out her keys and mobile phone. She locked the front door and dialled for Nick as quick as she could.

"Hey, Martha. I only dropped you off 10 minutes ago, can't get enough of me already?" Nick answered with his usual confidence.

"Nick, I need you to come back, now!" Her voice was shaky and her breathing was heavier than usual.

"Why, what's wrong?"

"Someone has been in my place. They broke in, left a note. Someone's after me, Nick!"

"Okay, okay. Just slow down. I'm on my way now and I'm going to call back up. Just stay calm. Is the intruder still there?"

"No, no it's just me. The person was in my bedroom! They cut my house phone!"

"I'll be there in 10 minutes. I'll be as quick as I can!" The phone line went dead and Martha collapsed into her sofa, skin prickled with goosebumps and her heart still beating 10 to the dozen.

Nick handed over a hot cup of tea to Martha as 10 officers searched her apartment.

"Thanks." Her hands were still trembling as she forced a smile.

Nick came and sat beside her on the cream coloured sofa and took a deep breath. "How are you feeling now?" The break-in happened around an hour ago and the officers were finishing up their search, the flashing of photographs being taken finally coming to an end.

"A bit shaky. I don't think I'll be sleeping for a long time."

"Do you have any idea who it could have been?"

"No. I couldn't even catch a glimpse." She placed her tea on the coffee table in front of the sofa. "Why would anyone do this? What does the note even mean? Am I in danger now?"

"No, of course not. " Nick placed a hand on Martha's right knee.

"It said it's his turn to torture me, that's a threat. I'm in danger!" Her voice was shaky and she clasped her head into her palms, resting both elbows against her knees prompting Nick to move his hand to her back.

"You're not in danger because I'm going to look after you. I'm not going to let some sleaze bag hurt you. They'll have to get past half a dozen officers and me before anyone even comes close to harming a hair on your head!"

"Excuse me," Luke Warring from the Burglary Specialist Unit (BSU) stood beyond the coffee table with both hands clasped behind his back.

"Yes?" Nick and Martha spoke simultaneously.

"We will be leaving shortly and I'll get my team to examine the evidence we found."

"What evidence was there?" Martha sat up straight.

"Well, it was a well thought out attack that took place."

"Meaning?"

"Not much was found, and what we did find may not be much help."

"Stop beating around the bush and fucking tell me!"

"There are no signs of a break-in or forced entry. He left through your bedroom window and we believe that is the way he came in as there was a small patch of fresh mud on your carpet, but it didn't even create a partial footprint. The house phone was cut off with wire cutters which anyone can get a hold of. No fingerprints or hairs were found anywhere in this flat other than those belonging to you. The note will hopefully help us find out whether our intruder was left or right-handed, assuming he was the one who wrote this."

"What's that supposed to mean?"

"The person who 'broke in' may have just been the messenger, so what evidence the note does give us won't help much in finding who the threat actually comes from."

"Great," she placed her head back into her hands.

"I'll leave you both to it. We'll be out in 5." Luke walked away and began helping his colleagues pack up and leave.

"It's my fault," Martha stuttered, then sniffed up through her running nose.

"That's not true and you know it isn't!" Nick pulled her into the sitting up position.

"It is. I left my window open when I wasn't home. If I closed and locked it then none of this would ever have happened!"

"Maybe not, but there would still be someone out there wanting to scare the shit out of you whether you left an opening to your home or not! Heck, they could have left the note on your front door or through your letterbox if they wanted, or sent it to your office at work. At least now you know to keep everything locked up and secured, you now know to report anything suspicious and I can now make sure no one comes after you. None of this was your fault. It's just some sick, twisted bastard playing mind games!" He wiped away her tears and pulled her into a reassuring hug. "You can take as much time off work as you need. You are your own priority and you need to keep safe."

"No," she pulled back and grabbed her cup of tea. "I need to work. It will keep me distracted from all this shit."

"Are you sure?"

"Yes. There is no way in hell am I staying here staring at the walls like a sitting duck. I want to work. We have a murder and rape to solve, no mother fucking dickhead is going to stop me from giving peace to the victims and families that need it, and punishment to those arseholes who deserve it." She took a big gulp from her tea.

"That's my girl," he gave her a wink and half a smile. "I'm not letting my eyes off you though. You can stay at mine until this blows over."

"I can't put you out like that. I'd be a nuisance. I'm fine here."

"Don't be so stupid. You're not a nuisance and never will be. You're not fine here because there may be some unwanted eyes staring this place down, and it is certainly not putting me out."

"It wouldn't be fair. I'm not your problem."

"You do not understand what I'm saying, do you? This isn't an offer. It's a demand. You're staying at mine whether you like it or not, and I'm going to have security at all entrances to my home. I need to make sure you're safe, it's my job, and I'm going to do it the best way I possibly can. You finish your tea while I go pack a few of your things."

"Thank you so much. I really don't know what I would do without you."

Nick stood, "what can I say, we're best friends. I'm not letting anything happen to you." He began to walk towards her bedroom.

"My away bag is in the bottom draw of my wardrobe. And don't forget to pack my underwear! And don't even think about bagging the mini dresses!"

"Haha, gotcha. I'll try my best to make you proud."

Martha smiled to herself as she watched Nick enter her room. *Such a lovely man. I could just kiss that face a million times over. No! You're just overwhelmed by shock. He's your best friend and colleague, nothing more.* She took a sip of her drink and a deep breath. The last of the officers had left and the apartment was now more or less empty.

* * *

Martha and Nick sat together in his home, the fire gently crackling beside them with the lights on dim. The sofa was white with soft cushions that gave the feeling of a warm embrace upon sitting. The laminate flooring was partially covered with a white rug that caressed one's toes with each step, pushing in softly under pressure and rising back to perfection after release. The home followed through with the white design, but still gave off warmth and welcome.

Nick placed his cup of hot chocolate on a coaster that sat on the lightly coloured coffee table in front of them. Martha continued to sip hers.

"Any ideas who it could be?" Nick hadn't stopped asking Martha questions about the home intrusion since they left her place.

"I've already told you, none."

"Do you have anyone who hates you?"

"Only everyone I've ever arrested!" Nick raised an eyebrow in a way to say he was only trying to help. "Sorry, I've just had enough thinking about someone who is out to get me. Can we talk about something else? At least until morning."

"Alright, talk to me."

"About what?"

"Our case."

"What about it?"

"We both know this hits close to home with you, and I don't want you

26

to be taking on something you can't cope with, especially now you've even more on your plate of worries."

Martha placed her cup next to Nick's.

"I'm fine working this case. Yes, I got a bit emotional talking to the mother, but it won't happen again. I swear."

"Then please, talk to me."

"I've told you about it before. There's nothing more to it."

"I've known you for years and I know when you're hiding something from me. Please, I'm here for you and I always will be. Just, please, for your own sanity stop bottling things up."

"It's not easy to talk about."

"I know. But the more I understand how you're feeling, the more I can help you and support you through this case." Nick leant his arms on his knees, sitting toward Martha.

"It's there, every day, in my head. The stench of alcohol on his breath, the prickly feel of his dried hands against my body, my waist. I can still see it now, pushing him, begging him to leave me alone. Didn't even know who he was. He just came out of nowhere and dragged me into the alley, I guess similar to Lisa Marsh. I try my hardest to forget the entire day. My 19th. Needless to say why I can't celebrate my birthday anymore; I mean, how can you celebrate the day your life was torn to pieces?" She wiped a tear from her eye and tried steadying her hands and voice.

Nick moved closer to her and wrapped an arm over her shoulders and pulled her into a tight hug, "I'm sorry."

"No, no. You're right. I need to open up to someone, and you're all I've got." She sat back up straight and wiped away the rest of her tears, picking up her hot chocolate and taking another sip. "I felt like my entire world had been turned upside down. I couldn't get my head around it. Why me? Was it my fault? Was I wearing too short a dress?" She sniffed. "Anyway, I knew deep down it wasn't my fault. It shouldn't

27

matter what you wear, no means no! But I still blamed myself. I felt dirty and sick. My legs struggled so much to hold me I didn't think I'd be making it home. I couldn't even think straight, I should have gone to the police then and there but I was too scared, too shocked. It's one of those things where you are so sure it would never happen to you, but it did. I was naive to think it wasn't possible and it was only something you hear about on the news."

"But it wasn't your fault! You just remember that!" Nick held tightly onto Martha's left hand.

"I get nightmares about it. Wake up in a cold sweat. When I finally reported it, it was too late to do anything. I didn't know my attacker, I didn't see him. I just felt him violating every inch of my body, stealing my privacy, my dignity, myself."

"How long did you wait to report it?"

"A year. I reported it on my 20th. Exactly a year. No evidence it ever happened, no description of the attacker, no witnesses. I left it too long. That - leaving him to get away and possibly find another victim - that was my fault!" She gritted her teeth and screwed her eyes, then looked back at Nick, forcing a brave smile.

"What made you report it?"

"Myself. The hate and anger and blame I threw upon me every day. The pain I inflicted on myself mentally, physically draining me and letting that son of a bitch ruin the rest of my life. I just wish I didn't torture myself for so long. I wish I didn't torture myself at all! I wish I reported him as soon as he ran off like the coward he was!" She finished the last of her hot chocolate, kissed Nick on the cheek and headed for the stairs for bed.

"I'm always here for you. I'm sorry I was never around when it happened." He stood by the sofa and Martha turned toward him.

"It made me who I am today. It helped me realise that I can make a difference and help get these scumbags off the street! And then I met you." She smiled. "I just wish the reason for me wanting to join the force wasn't rape." She climbed the rest of the stairs and headed straight for the spare room.

"Me too." He switched off the lights.

CHAPTER FIVE

Martha's mobile was ringing on the bedside table. She turned over in the bed and looked at the time. 10:23 am. *Shit!* She leant over and answered.

"Hello?" She mumbled, eyes squinting and voice groggy.

"Hey, it's me, Tyler. You never called back about lunch or dinner, what's up?"

"Oh!" She sat up in bed and rubbed her left palm down her face. "I am so sorry! I've had so much on my mind, what with this new case and last night, and now I'm late – "

"Woah there! Back up!" She cut through. "What do you mean last night? What happened?"

"It's a long story, and I'm late for work."

"You're never late to work. Did you get drunk or something?"

"Oh, I wish. Look, how about we meet for lunch around 1 at Wether-spoons, we can catch up then."

"Yeah sounds cool. See you there!" The phone went dead.

10:26. *Why the fuck did Nick not wake me?* She pulled herself out of bed and hurried around the spare room, pulling on a white blouse, black fitted trousers and a blazer jacket. She quickly slipped on her flats, ran down the stairs and grabbed her keys and coat before dashing out of the door. *Looks like a Public Transport kinda day!*

* * *

Martha barged through the entrance doors to the MSMI floor, swiping her card on the tab near the reception desk as she rushed past, and opened up the second set of doors into the main bureau. She spotted Nick just closing their office door and walked over to him quickly.

"Nick!" She gasped angrily but quietly.

"Oh hey, Martha. What are you doing here?"

"Well not working, that's for sure. Why the hell didn't you wake me this morning?"

"After the night you had, the department thought it best to give you the rest of the week off to help recuperate." He opened the door to their office and they both walked in, closing it behind them.

"Recuperate? The heck do I need to recuperate! Who the hell would take my place on our case?"

"Taz said she'd step in until you feel fit enough to return."

"Taz? You mean the slime-ball slut who tried stealing my job last year? The same Taz who tries getting into every man's bed that she can? The Taz who is daughter to our boss, Mohammad? That Taz?" She sat heavily into her chair and took a deep breath and let it out.

"Yes, that Taz." He paused for a minute and then continued. "Look, I know you don't like her but right now she is trying to be there for you."

"Well take this on board; I'm fit enough to return, I was never unfit in the first place. All that happened last night was someone trying to scare the shit out of me. Now, I would like to continue working like nothing ever happened, and if - and that's a big *if* – if I need a break then feel free to get someone in for the time being, but I do *not* want it to be Taz! She's a self-righteous, back-stabbing-"

The door to their office opened and Tazmin Muskhan stood in the doorway.

"-lovely person." Martha finished.

"Hey, Marth!" She said with a sly smile.

"It's Martha." She corrected her.

"Yeah, no need to keep reminding me. Anyhow, weren't expecting you back for some time."

"Well, it looks like I didn't need the break anyway, but thank you for offering to help."

"Yeah, offering Nick, not you."

"Is there a reason for you trespassing into my office?"

"Actually there is. I got some news about Nick's case."

"Well thank you," Martha stood up and walked around the desk to take the folder in Taz's hand. "I'll take that and have a look through."

"I was going to give it to Nick!" She tried pulling it back, but Martha's grip was tighter and pulled it away first, walking back round to her desk.

"Taz, it's alright. She's my partner. Whether you like it or not, she needs a look at the case files too. I'll catch you later."

"Yeah, later." She smiled peacefully at Nick, sent a sarcastic smile in the direction of Martha, then left the office and shut the door behind her.

"God knows how she hasn't been fired yet! Bloody pathetic and childish!"

"Yes, but given her dad is the head of the department, I doubt her losing her job will happen any time soon," Nick said, taking a seat on the opposite side of Martha's desk. "So what do we have?"

Martha opened the case file and read through. "Well, looks like we've found the exact location she was working, so we can interview them. The sperm found at the scene hasn't been matched to anyone on our Database, but it is still currently being cross-checked with other records on file and from across the sea just in case. We also may have a lead on the possible boyfriend and his whereabouts. We have a Jason Stark, 27, unemployed, previous records of shoplifting, a fine for assault last year and about 5 years ago he was reported for domestic abuse, but then the statement was withdrawn. The partner, who reported the crime but then claimed she was lying for attention was Lisa Marsh, aged 19."

"Well, looks like a possible suspect to me. But if they've been in a relationship for so many years, how could her mum not know? She struggled to remember his name and never told us about any domestic troubles her daughter could have been in." Nick took the file from Martha and began flicking through.

"Personally, I think we should question them both. No reports took place after the initial one 5 years ago, and if Lisa was lying for attention or telling the truth, Jason doesn't sound like the kind of guy you'd forget about after hanging around your daughter for so many years."

"I'm with you on this one. We'll get lunch, head to the mother's house, and then after that, we'll head to the boyfriend's, hopefully with more information about his life with Lisa."

"Sounds like a plan. Meet you back here at 1, I'll move my lunch plans forward."

"Date?"

"With an old friend".

"Right. Do I know him?"

"I'm joking, it's not a date, and it's a female friend." She stood and began heading toward the office door.

"Yeah well, I knew that. Anyway, none of my business if you have a date with a man." He stood and left the room first, waiting for Martha to exit.

"Well, never you mind. You'll be the first person I tell if I ever get a date!"

"Glad to hear it. Pick you up in an hour." He walked off as she locked their office door and started for the exit.

You just can't see it, can you Nick? She left.

* * *

"So, you gonna tell me what happened last night?" Tyler finished the last of her chips as Martha washed her food down with a gulp of ice-cold coke.

Feeling the drink slither down into the pit of her belly, Martha let out a small and reluctant sigh. "I had some guy break in through my bedroom window, left a note on my door. I got home before he made it out."

"Shit! Did he hurt you? Do you know who he was?" She leant forward in her seat and placed her arms upon the dining table.

"No idea who he was. Never got to see his face. He ran before I could do anything, which I guess is lucky in a way because it meant I got out unharmed."

"Bloody hell! What did the note say?"

"That it was his turn to torture me or something."

"What on earth does that mean?"

"I guess it means he wants to hurt me for something I've done, but what that could be I have no idea. Could be someone I've arrested, could just be some nutcase. Either way, he had the chance then and there to hurt me; I walked straight into his arms pretty much, so why did he run?"

"Probably scared of you?"

"Then why leave a note to threaten me if he hasn't got the balls to act on it?"

"Some things you just can't find answers to, hun. But look on the bright side, while he's leaving you alone that means you can get on with living your life. He seems to me all talk and no action, and that's nothing to complain about when the topic is your safety."

"I guess you're right. What's the point in looking over my shoulder

34

like a scared little girl if all he has is words to threaten me with! I've got a case to run and there is no damn son of a bitch that's going to stop me!"

"That's the Martha I know!" She chuckled.

"So, sister from another Mister, you got any big stories I haven't caught up with yet?"

"There is one. In fact, it's the reason why I wanted to meet up with you."

"Oh?" She frowned and leant forward slightly, gesturing for Tyler to continue.

"Well," Tyler leant back in her chair and rubbed both hands gently across her stomach, "I'm pregnant." She smiled.

"No way!" Martha could hardly contain her squeal of joy. "Oh my god, Tyler! That's amazing news! How far gone are you?"

"About 14 weeks."

"Oh, Tyler that's absolutely wonderful! I am so happy for you! What about the man of the house?"

"Derek? Bragging to all his mates about how brilliantly skilled his sperm is. God knows where I picked that one up from!"

"I am so happy for both of you! I always knew motherhood would come your way. You'll be an amazing mum!"

"And you'll be an amazing Godmother." She winked at Martha.

"What? Are you serious?" Suppressing the smile of joy was too hard.

"Of course I'm serious! Who better to be my child's Godmother than the woman who is pretty much my sister? I love you to pieces girl, and God forbid anything happens to me, I know my baby will have a great mother in you!"

A tear fell from Martha's right eye and she quickly wiped it away. She stood and hurried around the dining table and gave Tyler a hug.

"Mind you don't squeeze me too hard! You'll end up forcing the baby out!" Martha released Tyler and slapped her on the arm.

"I'm honoured, Tyler. I will be the best Auntie this kid will ever know!"

"I'm sure you will."

Martha's phone began to ring. Nick. "Give us a sec, gotta take this." She stood over to the side slightly and answered. "Y'ello?"

"Whereabouts are you?" The engine of the car was obvious in the background.

"Just finishing up at Wetherspoons, why?"

"I'll pick you up from there, will be outside in 5."

"Is everything okay?"

"Not really. Somehow the first DNA test on the semen was messed up in the process. Dave can't seem to understand how the sample was contaminated but something happened. He carried out the test again and this time we got something."

"So we have a match after all?"

"Not quite."

"Oh?"

"There seems to be two sets of DNA on the victim. One of them we have a match for. Scotty Branning, a well-known drug addict."

"So we're heading to him instead of the mum and boyfriend?"

"He's dead!"

"What? How?"

"They're thinking another murder, but we won't know for sure until Jessica comes back with the autopsy report."

"Do they think it's linked?"

"It's looking like it. I got to go because I'm expecting a call back from David. He thinks he may be onto how the samples were ruined. I'll be there to pick you up in a bit. Sorry to be cutting your lunch short."

"It's fine. See you in a bit." She hung up the phone and put it into her pocket, picking up her jacket from the chair she was sat on for lunch.

"I'm so sorry Tyler but that was work. It seems something urgent has come up."

"Hey, it's fine. We got our lunch together. We can catch up properly this weekend?"

"Yeah. That would be great!"

Tyler stood from her chair and hugged Martha. "Go catch 'em, girl! I'll be waiting!"

Martha did a little wave to Tyler's belly and walked to the exit smiling. *A Godmother, an Auntie! Nothing can ever ruin this!* She left.

CHAPTER SIX

"**S**o, what happened?" Martha asked climbing into Nick's Mazda.

"David Mace was to carry out the DNA test on the semen. When he received the first lot of samples he found that they had all been tampered with." He started the engine and began to drive.

"How so?"

"I had David text what happened. When he told me over the phone I knew there was no way I could remember what he said." He kept a hand on the wheel while pulling his phone from his pocket with the other, handing it over the Martha.

"Right," she unlocked the phone and clicked onto the most recent message. David Mace.

'*Someone within the MSMI Department or the DNA Lab found a way to damage the semen samples sent to me from the victim. It seems someone got their hands on a substance called DNase. DNase is an enzyme that catalyses the hydrolytic cleavage of phosphodiester connections in the DNA's backbone, thus degrading the sample. Thankfully the second lot of samples I ordered were not damaged. There are two sets of DNA found, meaning there were two men who attacked Lisa closer to the time she was murdered. Only one set was on file, revealing the attacker as Scotty Branning who has recently been found deceased. Jessica Heath is currently working on the cause of death.'*

"I don't think I understand half of that!" She locked the phone and put it to rest in the cupholder between the two of them.

"What I take from that is there is either a dirty cop in our midst or someone really fucked up at the lab. I'm hoping it was the latter, though I doubt we will find out any time soon."

"So where're we off to now?

"I say, boyfriend. Let him know about Lisa if her mum hasn't already given him the news. See if he knows anything else about this that we don't."

"Not liking the boyfriend, no?"

"Going by his records? I wouldn't trust him as far as I could throw him." Silence consumed the vehicle as they continued the journey to Jason Stark's home.

* * *

After arriving outside Jason Stark's home – a block of high raised flats - Martha and Nick pulled themselves from the car, made their way up the littered path to the run-down building and took the only working lift up to the 13th floor. They found the place they were looking for with black bin bags taking up most of the ground space, causing a gut-wrenching stench of rotting food, faeces and weed to devour the air completely. They approached the front door, breathing through their mouths, and rang on the bell. After a few seconds, a man in his late twenties opened the door. Light brown hair, tanned skin – fake? – heavy brown eyes and a stubbly beard making a shy appearance through the flesh of his ageing face. He was wearing a grey tracksuit, *Nike*, something all too common in London and not the least bit smart. Jason Stark squinted at the two detectives and sighed, mist forming from the heat of his breath and rising into the excessively cold air.

"Yes?" He groaned.

"I'm Detective Nick Hardy, and this is my partner Detective Martha Willis. We work within the MSMI Institute of Law and we've come to speak with you about your partner, Lisa Marsh. Can we come in, please?" His words were bold and authoritative. Nick had this one.

"What's the bitch done now?" he growled.

"She was raped and murdered, Mr Stark," Nick replied.

His face twisted with anger, but there was a hint of shock and horror in his eyes. "You what?"

"Lisa Marsh was murdered and we need to talk to you as part of our ongoing investigation."

"Look, that has fuck all to do with me, so why don't you both just do one?" He went to slam the door, but it stopped just short of closing. Looking down in confusion and frustration, he saw Nick's foot blocking the door. "What do you think you're playin' at?" He began to raise his voice.

"If you do not let us in I will have to arrest you for obstructing a police investigation. What will it be, Mr Stark?" Nick's face was stern and his hand had moved to hold the side of the door, Martha not having memory of this movement taking place.

"Fine," he grunted reluctantly, opening the door fully once more to let the Detectives into his home.

Jason Stark led the way into his badly lit living room. The place reminded Martha of some kind of horror film, but she couldn't quite place her finger on which film. Nevertheless, the flat gave her immense anxiety.

Jason collapsed back into his armchair, reaching for a can of John Smiths from the stained coffee table on his way down. Nick gave a disapproving look, with only a quick raise of Jason's left eyebrow and his beer in reply.

"Where were you on Monday the 9th of January?" Nick asked sternly.

"Is that when she was murdered?" Despite asking, his voice seemed to show no interest in what the answer would be, and his eyes stared at the detectives coldly.

"That's when she went missing," Martha answered.

"Dumb bitch got lost in her home town?" He sniggered.

"Just answer the question!" Nick snapped.

"Hm, let me think." Pause. "I was at work from 9 till 5. Car repair shop down the road."

"Before 9?"

"Asleep. Woke up at 10 to, ran there still pulling on my shirt."

"And after 5?"

"Fuck this interrogation man, I ain't got shit to do with this!"

"Where were you on Monday the 9th of January after 5, Mr Stark?" Nick's voice was low and serious. He clearly didn't have time for Jason's attitude.

"Shit man, I spent the night with some slut, here, all fucking night!"

"Whose?"

"Olivier Carmen. Smoked some shit and fucked the bird, alright?" He pushed himself out of his armchair in a huff, slamming his beer on his small coffee table. "You gonna check if we really fucked?"

"I'm going to check if your alibi is true, yes." Nick walked toward the doorway and pulled out his phone and dialled. "Yes, it's Detective Nick Hardy. Could you pull the number for an Olivier Carmen, please? Thank you." He put the phone down and proceeded to stare at the screen.

PING!

He began to dial again, and then put the phone to his ear.

"Hello, is that Olivier Carmen? Yes, this is Detective Nick Hardy. I work for the MSMI Department from the UK National Criminal Law

Bureau, I was wondering if I could confirm the whereabouts of a Mr Jason Stark on Monday the 9th of January?" Pause, deep breath, sigh. "He claims you were together in the evening after 5, could you confirm this? Right. Okay. Thank you." He hung up and put the phone back into his pocket. Another sigh. He turned and walked back into the room.

"Well?" Jason pushed.

"It turns out his alibi checks out. Not that she was happy admitting to sleeping with a cheating jerk."

"You what?" Jason puffed his bare chest out and pushed it toward Nick, something prime animals do in order to look bigger when in the face of danger.

"Not my words, kid!" Nick pushed him away and held his right hand up in warning. "Do you have an alibi for Sunday the 22nd of January? And the 21st?"

"How the fuck am I supposed to remember?"

"It was the day your girlfriend was killed and the morning her fucking body was found! Now answer my fucking question!"

"I guess. I was at the pub with some of the lads, not that it's any of your fucking business!"

"We'll be checking with the Landlord if that's true. For now, you're free from being locked up; but don't think I won't change my mind. Now can my partner and I leave here in peace, or am I going to have to arrest you for assaulting an officer?"

"Fuck off!" He stormed into what the Detectives believed to be the kitchen, and so they made their way to the exit.

Finding themselves back in Nick's Mazda, the Detectives shared a sigh and a welcomed silence. The engine was running with the heaters on to battle the cold bite of winter's air.

"I was really hoping his alibi wouldn't be confirmed," Nick complained.

"Tell me about it. What a nasty piece of work. Although with an attitude like that, I'm surprised Lisa's mother couldn't remember such an awful boyfriend."

"We might have to pay her another visit. I would certainly remember if my daughter was dating an abusive piece of scum like him. I hope she isn't trying to cover for his behaviour by pretending she'd forgotten him. For now, though, I think it's time to write up our notes and head home." He put his car in gear and pulled away.

CHAPTER SEVEN

After being back at Nicks' for a little over two hours, Martha decided it was time to put herself to bed. As she lay in the spare room, she found her mind racing against her will.

That poor girl deserved so much better. Why was she with that guy? He must have treated her awfully. Why didn't her mum say anything? Stop her from seeing him? Surely she knew Jason was a horrible man, or at least saw something different in Lisa's behaviour. How was such a toxic relationship allowed to go on for so long? Was he physically abusive toward her?

Sleep was proving difficult, despite the immense exhaustion her body felt.

He seems like the type of person to attack someone. He doesn't seem to care about the law. Heck, he didn't give a fuck that Nick and I were detectives and indirectly asking if he was a murderer. In his mind, he probably thought he was higher than us, that we had no authority over him. He may be innocent of abduction, but he is certainly guilty of being a self-obsessed prick!

As the night continued to draw in, Martha finally succumbed to the land of nod.

* * *

The bedroom door creaked. Martha's eyes blinked open. She couldn't see but dared not move. The room was dark, and her mind created swirls and faces in the blackness. *Is the door open, or closed?* Her breath became shallow, and the hairs on the back of her neck stood to attention, goosebumps prickling her flesh, heart pounding loud enough to wake the neighbours. The door opened. Martha tried to sit up and face the person entering her temporary room, but her body grew stiff. The duvet held her against her will as she lay on the right side of her body, feet at the end, with her back facing against the window. The floorboards rattled, and heavy footsteps approached the bed, heading toward the window side. Martha attempted a scream for help, but her mouth dried up, her throat closed and swelled, her neck tightened. Something came up behind her. A hot breath brushed against her ear. At last, she forced out a cry.

"NICK!"

* * *

"Martha? Martha!" Nick ran into Martha's room, boxers the only clothing he was in. He turned on the light to Martha rolling around in bed, screaming, her eyes clamped shut and screwed. The room was otherwise empty. He ran to her bedside and grabbed a hold of both her shoulders and began to shake her. "Martha! Martha, it's me, Nick! You're dreaming! It's just a dream!"

Martha shot up, her breath heavy and fast, tears streaming down her face. "Nick, he was here, he was here!"

"It was a dream. A bad dream. You're safe, I promise." He pulled her into a tight and reassuring hug.

"Please don't leave me." She sobbed into his shoulder.

"I won't. I'm here. I'm not going anywhere." He began to cradle her. *I will never leave you.*

* * *

Nick drew the curtains open revealing a dull morning, and brought a mug of freshly brewed tea to Martha's bedside table. She stirred.

"Morning sleepyhead," Nick whispered gently.

"Hey, what time is it?" Her voice was groggy.

"Just gone ten. I called Taz and let her know we'll be late in."

"Why didn't you call Mohammad? He's the boss."

"I did, she answered. Turns out her dad's on vacation for a week and has left her in charge."

"Seriously? Of all people?"

"She's letting us come in late, Martha. She's not as bad as you think."

Martha shot up in the bed, Nick sitting on the edge by her side. "You didn't tell her what happened last night, did you?"

"Of course not!" He paused. "How are you feeling?"

"Headache, tired. But ok, I guess."

"So what happened?"

"I think it's the break-in playing on my mind. I didn't even know I was asleep. I was sure it was real." She picked up her tea from the bedside table and blew it before taking a sip. "A man came in."

"Did you see who it was?"

"No. I couldn't move."

"Do you think it was a man who broke into your home?"

"I'm certain. A man broke in. I know it was just a dream, but there was something about the man. Whoever it was, I'm sure it was the same man, too." They both sat in silence, Martha drinking her tea, Nick

46

staring at his feet on the ground, thinking.

"I believe you. If your gut thinks it was a man, then so do I!" Martha smiled for the support Nick was giving her. The detectives went on to finish their teas and then left for work.

* * *

Martha and Nick pulled up outside Miss Marsh's house. Baby snowflakes fell like feathers from the sky, evaporating after their gentle landings on the pavement.

"You sure you alright to work?" Nick asked.

"It helps keep my mind occupied. Anyway, it was only a stupid dream." She sighed.

"Ready?"

"Ready." She nodded. They both got out of the car.

Nick rang on the doorbell. The detectives shared a glance, and then the door finally cracked open.

"Yes?" Miss Marsh croaked.

"Hello, Miss Marsh. It's Detective Nick Hardy and Detective Martha Willis. Do you remember? Nick asked.

"Um, I think. Do you have IDs?"

Nick and Martha shared a confused glance, then pulled their badges from their coats and showed them to Miss Marsh who opened the door wider.

"Ah, yes, I see." She grumbled. "Come in." The invite inside didn't come soon enough for Martha, as her fingers grew so cold that she could barely move them, and her nose glowed bright red.

Finding themselves back in the familiar home of Miss Marsh, the detectives took a seat in her living room as she bought two freshly made cups of tea.

"Thank you." They said simultaneously as they took their drinks from the old lady.

"Have you found my Lisa?" Miss Marsh finally asked as she took a seat in her armchair.

"Pardon?" Martha grew more confused.

"My Lisa, she went missing two weeks ago. Have you found her?"

"Miss Marsh," Nick began. "Lisa went missing around 25 days ago. Do you remember?"

"No, you're wrong. It's been two weeks."

A young man in pale blue jeans and a black T-Shirt walked into the room. "Guests?"

Nick stood up. "I'm Detective Nick Hardy, and this is my partner, Detective Martha Willis," he gestured as Martha stood up, and put out his left arm for a handshake.

"I see. I'm Kevin Linn, Lillian Marsh's carer." Kevin snubbed the friendly introduction and flared his nostrils. Nick rolled his eyes and put his hand back down by his side.

"Carer?" Martha asked.

"Yes. Lillian has Alzheimer's."

"We had no idea! You weren't here on our last visit."

"I don't work with her every day, I'm afraid. Of course, due to her memory, I had no idea who you were and that you'd made a visit previously."

"How serious is it?" Nick asked, and the three sat on the sofa while Lillian Marsh drank her tea in her armchair.

"Quite. It has gotten worse in the past month or so." He paused. "Why are you here?"

"Miss Marsh's daughter was found exactly two weeks after she went missing."

"That's great!"

"Not exactly," Nick interrupted, raising his eyebrows.

"Oh, I see. How awful." His voice remained monotonous despite the situation.

"Initially we came to update Miss Marsh on the investigation and to ask a few more questions."

"I can try and help where I can?"

"That would be lovely, thank you." Martha took the lead. "We spoke to Lisa's boyfriend. It seems he was rather rough with her, but he has an alibi that has checked out, so he is out of the picture."

"And the questions?"

"Well, we wanted to know why Miss Marsh struggled to remember someone who was so abusive towards her daughter, and how she didn't bring this to light during our initial visit; but now I believe our questions have been answered."

"I see." Kevin sighed and twiddled his fingers.

"Is my Lisa okay?" Miss Marsh asked, her hands shaking.

"I think, if all questions are answered, it is time that you both leave." Kevin stood up, followed by the detectives.

"Thank you for your time. I'm sorry if we've caused any inconveniences or distress." Nick shook his hand.

"That's okay. I have to get back to my job now, and explain what has happened with Lisa."

"Thank you," Martha whispered, and the detectives left the warmth of the old house and became one with the cold air again.

They sat in the car, heating on full. The sky began to summon dark clouds above them, and small specks of snow kissed the floor once again.

"Well, I wasn't expecting that." Martha sighed.

"Neither was I." He agreed. "Alzheimer's. Bloody hell."

"We've hit a dead-end again. Boyfriend has an alibi, and the mother has Alzheimer's so wasn't covering anything up. Where do we look now?"

"We'll visit Lisa's boss. Ready?"

"I guess."

Nick put the car into gear and drove off.

CHAPTER EIGHT

"Hey, I'm **Mark Donald, manager of Aldi,**" he shook Nick's hand, and then Martha's. "How can I help you?"

The three of them sat in the back office of Aldi, the cold air pinching at their skins, hairs standing on end.

"We're here to ask questions about one of your employees, Lisa Marsh," Nick said.

"Oh, yes! Great worker, until she went missing."

"We'd like to know how much you can tell us about the last time you saw her?"

"I can't remember the date, but it was the day before her mother reported her missing."

"That would be Sunday the 8th," Martha confirmed.

"Yes. She was working a few hour shifts, finished at 5. Haven't seen her since."

"How did she seem to you?" Nick asked.

"Normal, I guess. Although she did have a nasty black eye. She said she walked into a cupboard, but between you and me, I think it was that bastard boyfriend of hers."

"And where were you on the 9th?"

"I was working here. You can check CCTV if you wish." He crossed his left leg over his right.

"If you don't mind. We might be able to work out who was around and if she spoke to anyone before she went missing."

"I have a question. I'm afraid I already know the answer, but I don't want it to be true." Mark stuttered.

"What's that?" Martha replied.

"Why are the MSMI on the case?"

"Lisa was found almost two weeks ago."

"Was she . . ." he couldn't bring himself to finishing the question.

"I'm afraid so." Martha sighed.

"I bet you it was that dickhead boyfriend of hers! You have to check him out, at least!"

"I'm afraid we already have, and his alibi has checked out" Nick chipped in.

"Fuck! Can you not arrest him for abuse?"

"Unfortunately not, due to no evidence proving it was him abusing her. I'm sorry."

"Fuck sake! I know it's not your fault but the law seriously pisses me off sometimes. You can clearly see he was abusive with all the injuries she sustained throughout their relationship. She even reported him and bailed when he threatened to kill her! I told her to get away from him but she didn't listen!"

"He threatened to kill Lisa?" Martha pushed.

"Yeah! But that was like forever ago."

"We did see she filed a report against him, but no further action was taken." Nick paused, then breathed out heavily. "Thank you for your time, Mr Donald. We'll be in touch if we have any further enquiries."

"No problem, Detective. I hope you find the son of a bitch who did this!"

Martha and Nick left the office and headed back outside into the bitter cold.

* * *

Martha sat on the edge of her bed in Nick's home, watching as dark clouds consumed the night sky. Flashes of her dream pricked at her eyes, the man breathing over her as she lay trapped in bed. The bathroom door on the landing opened and Nick stepped out, then looked through the bedroom door to Martha.

"Bathroom is free."

"Thank you."

"Are you okay?" He frowned.

"Yeah, just tired."

"Make sure you get a good night's rest. See you in the morning."

"Yeah, see ya." She sighed as Nick walked toward his own room at the end of the landing. She pulled herself up from the bed and made her way to the bathroom to ready herself for the night ahead.

CHAPTER NINE

Martha awoke to her phone vibrating intensely. She rolled over and answered. "Hello?"

"Hello, Martha. It is Jessica from the forensic team. Is now a good time?"

"Yeah, sure. What's up?" She pulled herself into an upright position and swung her legs over the side of her bed.

"I have the reports back on the partial footprint left in your apartment."

"Right . . ."

"The size of the shoe was around 9½ , and with the print on the carpet being even, I can confirm the person was wearing the right-sized shoes due to the weight distribution."

"Come again?" Nick walked into the room at this point, knocking on the bedroom door lightly with two of his knuckles. Martha put her index finger to her lip and then signalled 1 minute.

"The intruder's shoe size is 9½ which narrows down our pool of suspects."

"And how will knowing the intruder's shoe size help us?"

"Statistics prove that the average male shoe size in the UK is 9, whereas the average for a female is around 6. With this footprint confirming our intruder was a size 9½, I would say the offender was almost certainly a man."

"How certain?"

"12% of the male population have a size 9½, the female population with a size of 9 and above makes just 1%. I would say I am 99% certain we are looking for a man."

"Thank you. I'll pass the information onto my team. Do you have anything else?"

"Yes, actually. From the sample taken from the print, I can confirm that the mud was from surrounding areas. What I found most interesting, though, was that small traces of gravel was also found. Gravel that matches that of the car park just across the road from your apartment."

"So I might be able to find evidence of him being there and maybe even a DNA sample if he left something like a cigarette butt on the ground?"

"There is some chance we could find something. Would you like me to call the National Criminal Law Bureau and send a unit over now?"

"Yes, yes! Absolutely! I'll be over shortly. Meet you there?"

"See you there, yes."

"Thank you!" She hung up the phone as Nick sat down beside her, topless, muscles prominent in his soft and beautiful flesh. Water trickled gently down his slightly tanned abs, his dark hair ruffled and wet from the shower he had just come from.

"You going to give me the good news, or will I have to beat it out of you?" He smirked.

"That was Jessica Heath from the forensics team. They've confirmed the shoe size of my intruder was 9½, meaning the probability of the unsub being a male is through the roof!"

"Your gut was right, then?"

"That's not even the best bit! They've found traces of gravel in the print that match the gravel in the car park I use. He might have left some more evidence behind which could lead us to finding who he is!"

"Then what are we waiting for, sitting here and chatting away?" He got up and winked at Martha. "Get ready then! We have a scene to attend."

Yes, boss! She smirked and let out a small chuckle of delight and excitement. *Maybe soon this will all be over!*

* * *

Martha and Nick watched on as Jessica's forensic team from the NCLB traced through every inch of the car park, dressed in all white bodysuits that Martha believed were probably waterproof. She stood there biting at the skin around her nails. She was also shaking, but not through the bitter, cold air, but nerves. *Please find something. Please!*

"What time is it?" She asked, her voice strained due to her dried up mouth.

"Erm . . ." Nick pulled the sleeve of his coat up to check his watch, then covered himself once again, shoving his hands into his pockets, clearly trying to fight against the cold. "Just gone 9. Don't worry, they'll be sure to document and test everything they find. Jessica has a good team here."

"But what if they miss one cigarette butt in all that gravel? The one butt that may have his DNA?"

"Jessica will be sure to leave no stone unturned."

"Funny." She sighed, blew on her hands, and then rubbed them together for warmth. "I can only hope he is a smoker and left some kind of trail behind him."

"Detective Willis!" Jessica called her over.

"Have you found something?" Martha replied as she got closer, Nick on her tail.

"We have found 5 cigarette butts. If we are lucky, and our guy is a smoker, one of these could have his DNA on it." 5 plastic bags sat on a set-me-up table, all with 1 butt in each.

"What happens next?"

"My team will continue searching through the parking lot. It is only a small space to cover, so we should not be too long. After that, I will take everything back to the lab with me and start looking for DNA evidence, and then finding whom they belong to. Once that is all done, it is down to you to bring our smokers in and begin questioning."

"Have you got anything back on the body of Scotty Branning?"

"I am expecting the toxicology results back today. I can confirm that he was in a fight before his death, but other than that I do not have any more information."

"Toxicology?" Nick interrupted.

"Yes. We found a needle mark left in his arm, quite fresh. I took some samples to test what he injected and how much of it. As soon as I get the results back, I will send them all your way, as with this car park business."

"Thank you so much for doing this!" Martha sighed in relief.

"No problem. It is my job, after all." Jessica smiled.

"We appreciate it." Nick stepped in. He took a hold of Martha's right arm and gently pulled her away from the scene. "We'll let them finish up here. No point in waiting around when we have a job to do as well. You'll have the results back in no time."

"Thank you for coming with me."

"Always." They both retreated to Nick's Mazda, and then set off for the UK National Criminal Law Bureau.

* * *

Martha and Nick sat in their office, paperwork sprawled across both of their desks. A messy pile for Martha's stalking, another messy pile for the rape and murder case of Lisa Marsh, and finally, at the end of the desk, a short brief into the death of Scotty Branning, Toxicology report pending. Nick had just finished eating a ham sandwich when they heard a bleep from Martha's computer.

"Anything interesting?" Nick asked, basket-balling his rubbish into the silver bin by the door.

Pushing the piles of paperwork to one side, Martha opened up her emails. "Yes, actually." Nick walked around to her side of the desk and leant over her shoulder. "We've just received the CCTV footage from Mark Donald, so now we can finally check what happened at Lisa's work the last few days leading up to her disappearance."

"Brilliant. Let's hope we find something!"

"I'll forward the message through to you. We can both trail through the footage together."

"Sweet. See you in a few."

"See ya!" Nick walked out of the room and Martha forwarded the CCTV footage over to his email. Once the email was confirmed as sent, Martha logged out of her computer, picked up her laptop bag from the side of her chair, and then exited the office herself.

CHAPTER TEN

Martha and Nick met up in a larger office room with both their laptops and a cup of coffee each. In the centre of the room was a large rectangular desk with soft padded chairs surrounding it and tucked in at every angle. The walls were bland with only a few nicks and dents here and there, while a whiteboard occupied one wall, and two square windows occupied the other. The carpet was an off-white colour with the occasional spot of dried, rock-hard gum stuck to it. The room, however dull, had the sweet aroma of strawberries, to the delight of all officers who had to use the space every now and again. Above the desk, wired into the ceiling, was a fairly new projector, pointing toward the whiteboard in standby.

730 hours of surveillance had been cut down to 168 hours by the MSMI surveillance team, leaving Martha and Nick with one week of footage to trail through . . . the week leading up to Lisa Marsh's disappearance.

"Who would have thought we'd be spending hours on end surveying CCTV. I'm bloody knackered!" Nick sighed. "And yet we still have nothing."

"Beats being at home where someone is watching you, though."

A brief pause, and then . . .

"LOOK!" Martha almost jumped out of her seat. "Look at the reflection in the mirror!"

Both Nick and Martha stared at the round mirror positioned by the

CCTV camera. In the reflection was Lisa Marsh and her mother's carer, Kevin Linn.

"What are they doing?" Nick asked himself aloud.

"Looks like a pretty serious conversation they're having."

Kevin's arms were flailing around while his face was contorted with pure anger. Lisa looked as though she was trying to calm him down, her lips miming "I'm sorry". Kevin then flew into a rage and punched her, causing her to fall to the floor holding the side of her face, crying.

"What's the date of this footage?" Nick asked.

Martha checked the properties of the file. "The day before she went missing."

"Well well well, so our carer isn't very caring after all. I think we're going to need to pay him a second visit."

"I'll get an address for him. Meet me in your car in 15."

* * *

"1-5-2 Wetheral Drive," Martha told Nick as he started the engine.

"About 10 minutes from here. Let's go get this son of a bitch!"

The journey was mostly silent until they finally pulled up outside of Kevin's address. A block of flats. Flat 1, floor 5, room 2. The lifts were under maintenance leaving the Detectives no choice but to work their cardio and run 5 flights of stairs.

"I have a passionately beautiful hate for climbing stairs!" Martha said, gasping for air.

"Tell me about it!" A quick grin crossed his lips along with a sneaky wink.

Room 2 was just to the right of the stairs, and without hesitation, Nick immediately started banging on Kevin's front door. "Kevin, it's

Detective Nick Hardy from the MSMI, open up!"

No answer.

"KEVIN!" Nick repeated louder.

Nothing.

"It's looking like nobody is home." Martha sighed.

"Good job we had this warrant rushed through last minute to check out his property, then." Nick pulled out the warrant, handed it to Martha, and then started kicking the door until it eventually gave way.

"Excuse me!" An old woman called from the door of room 3. "What on Earth do you think you're doing? I'm going to call the police!" She yelped in fear.

"No need, MSMI, and we have a warrant." Martha pulled out her badge to show the old lady, and swiftly waved the warrant in the air.

"Now please, let us get back to work, otherwise you'll be done for obstructing officers of the law!" Nick snapped, before walking into Kevin's apartment. The old woman grunted with disgust at Nick's attitude, but proceeded to follow the instructions and went back into her flat.

The flat was dark and dingy with a putrid stench of urine, faeces, and weed. The mix of smells was horrific, causing Nick and Martha to turn up their noses. The kitchen and living room made one large room with a wooden brown coffee table placed right in the middle. The two sofas in the room were covered in rips and yellow stains. Nothing in the flat, not even pictures, were placed with care. Everything was haphazard. Upon the wooden coffee table was traces of white powder along with out-of-date bank cards scattered all around.

"I'm going to take a wild guess and assume cocaine." Martha sighed.

"We'll take some samples for the lab and seal off the apartment. Who knows what else we'll find in here." Nick headed into the bedroom to the right, not too long before calling his partner into the room.

As Martha walked in, she instantly knew what he was looking at. "Is that a shrine? A shrine for our victim?"

"Yup. Along with a lock of hair and a pair of knickers, no doubt belonging to Lisa."

"Wow, he's looking more and more innocent as the investigation grows," she replied sarcastically.

Before the conversation could continue, Kevin barged into the room. "What the fuck do you think you're doing in my home?!"

"Kevin, we're arresting you on suspicion of drug trafficking, kidnap and mur-"

Nick was cut off as Kevin made a dart for the exit.

"Fucking son of a bitch!" Nick grumbled before chasing after their newest suspect, pulling out his gun and radio. "NHMW calling dispatch, we need backup. The suspect is running, looks to be heading toward the underground. Cordon off the perimeter. The suspect is a possible danger to the public!"

Within minutes, sirens could be heard ringing around the block. Kevin weaved his way past multiple obstacles, throwing bins behind him as he pressed on, forcing Nick to jump over. Innocent bystanders saw themselves being shoved with one elderly woman losing her balance and collapsing on the floor. Nick refused to stop the chase. His heart was pounding and his chest was burning, but he eventually managed to catch up to the suspect, thus putting his gun into his sling and pouncing, bringing Kevin to the floor with a loud thud and a snapping noise from his wrist. Nick pulled Kevin's arms behind his back with force, a yelp of pure agony bursting from between his lips. His wrist was clearly broken, but Nick handcuffed him none-the-less.

"Kevin Linn, I am arresting you on the suspicions of drug trafficking, stalking, rape, and kidnap."

"You what?" Kevin screamed.

"You do not have to say anything, but it may harm your defence if you do not mention when questioned something which you may later rely on in court."

"You piece of shit! Get off me!"

"Anything you do say may be given in evidence. Now let's get your sorry arse in a cell where it belongs!" Nick pulled Kevin up to stand as a marked police car and a van pulled up. Pedestrians watched on in awe as Kevin was placed in the back of the police van and carted off.

* * *

While the chase was on, Martha welcomed CSI into Kevin's apartment and put up 'Crime Scene' tape at the front door in order to prevent trespassing. The team of CSI Agents came equipped with gloves, goggles, face masks, white plastic boots and jumpsuits; hairnets and a breathing apparatus, all to ensure that health and safety were met, as well as preserving the crime scene. Martha watched on as they began taking samples of the white powder left on the coffee table, while also bagging the pair of knickers that were found in the bedroom, and the bank cards that were all out of date. They also began searching the kitchen for a knife that could match what was used to assault Lisa.

A Crime Scene Photographer was taking pictures of the shrine which was surrounded by candles, fairy lights, and at least 250 photos of Lisa; some pinned up on the wall, others scattered on the desk directly below the shrine. After about 20 minutes, Martha's phone began to ring. Nick.

"Hello."

"I caught the son of a bitch. He's being taken to the Police Station ready for questioning. How's the crime scene coming along?"

"CSI are here and the area has been sealed off. I'll meet you downstairs and we'll drive back to the station. See how Kevin can explain this one away." Martha hung up the phone and proceeded to leave the scene.

CHAPTER ELEVEN

The police station was cold, dark, and damp, despite its sophisticated appearance; not the most pleasant of places to be spending the night, but that was exactly what Kevin was there to do. It was an old station, resulting in a heating system that had yet to be upgraded, windows that were clearly blown, and overnight cells covered in dirt.

The interrogation room. Warm, black walls, and a metal table in the middle, a vast contrast to the rest of the police station, following the theme of the new MSMI building down the road. Kevin stared across the table at Nick and Martha. His eyes were bloodshot and filled with rage, his face red, chest heaving, heavy breaths. He was in his early 30s, black-rimmed glasses, a missing front tooth, and light blonde hair. At the end of the table was a tape machine recording the entire interview.

"I swear to you, I didn't do anything!"

"Funny, because last I checked, innocent people don't run," Nick said.

"I ran because I knew you'd lock me up!"

"And why would we do that?" Asked Martha.

"The fucking drugs, man! Like you were gonna let me go for having cocaine all around my apartment."

"True, but we're not here for the cocaine. We're here in the regards of the kidnapping and murder of Lisa Marsh."

"Well, I didn't fucking kill her!

"But you were obsessed, no?" Nick interrupted.

"I was in love!"

"You see, that shrine in your bedroom tells me otherwise. Did Lisa know you had over 250 pictures of her? Including images of her dressing herself through the bedroom window? Because something tells me she had no idea you were stalking her."

"Look right, she loved me."

"She had a boyfriend," Martha added.

"She was going to break things off with him. He was abusive."

"And do you have proof of any of this? Or are you just trying to put the blame on someone who isn't yourself?"

"I cared for her mum. I cared for her!"

"You have a bloody shrine in your bedroom. That's an obsession, not care."

"Well think what you want, but I know I didn't kill her."

"Then why are you both seen on CCTV arguing in the stock room of Aldi?" Nick pressed on.

"That was just a disagreement. Nothing more."

"Quite a big disagreement if it resulted in you punching her so hard that she fell to the floor. Who was supposed to be the abusive one, her boyfriend or you?"

"I got angry, okay?" Kevin sighed heavily.

"Angry is an understatement." Nick spat.

"Why did you hit her?" Martha continued.

"She was going to pull out of dumping her scumbag boyfriend, that's why! She obviously loved being pushed around if she didn't want to leave Jason. So I hit her. I showed her I could be nasty too if I put my mind to it."

"How very kind of you," Nick replied sarcastically.

"I treated her like a princess and she was still going to leave me. She had it coming!"

"Something tells me she wasn't as fond of you as you were of her. You were stalking her; took pictures of her walking to and from work, pictures of her having a shower taken from outside of her own home, a place that should be safe and private. You took that away from her, and you plastered it all over your bedroom walls. She had no intention of being with you, Kevin, and so you raped and killed her!"

"That is not true! I could never do that. She was my life."

"She was your victim, Kevin! At no point was she ever your lover!" Martha protested.

"I want a lawyer!" He demanded. Nick reluctantly ended the interview and switched off the tape, and then both detectives left the interrogation room in a huff, clearly pissed off with their suspect and his inept grasp on reality.

* * *

"Kevin's lawyer is on his way," Tazmin informed Martha and Nick before returning to her desk. "Also, Jessica called. No knives were found to match the one that was used on Lisa. She's on her way down with some more info." And with that, Tazmin left the room.

"What are you thinking?" Martha asked her partner.

"That he is one fucked up mother fucking fruit loop."

"I don't think I could have put it any better. Jessica is currently examining the underwear we found in Kevin's flat. Hopefully, she can find something to help with our enquiries— Speak of the devil..."

Jessica walked over to Martha and Nick with a small file in her hands.

"Tell me you have something juicy." Nick pleaded.

"The underwear from Kevin's apartment seems to belong to our victim—"

"Son of a bitch!"

"But there are no signs of semen or any DNA from our suspect on them at all. And there is no evidence of Lisa ever stepping foot in the apartment."

"Then how do you know those are her undies?" Martha asked, completely puzzled.

"Traces of skin and hair follicles match the DNA of our victim."

"So how did they get in his apartment?"

"My guess is he stole them while caring for her mum," Nick grunted.

"What a sick and twisted individual. What about the powder?"

"100% cocaine. The credit cards had fingerprints belonging to more than one individual, so it is my guess that he was probably holding a drug-fuelled party with his mates."

"Does anything point to him killing and raping our victim?" Martha asked.

"Unfortunately, I cannot find anything that could link him to the murder and rape of Lisa."

"Fucking hell! Looks like we're either going to get a confession, or he'll be released once the mandatory 24 hours is up, and so far it's looking like the latter." Nick growled.

"Thank you, Jessica."

"Any time."

As Jessica left, Martha turned to her partner. "We have CCTV evidence and a confession from Kevin to hitting Lisa the day before she went missing. Maybe we could break him down a bit and see if he has any other confessions he wishes to make."

"If only he didn't call for his lawyer!"

* * *

Kevin sat smugly with his lawyer by his side, a smirk that Nick wanted to knock off his face.

"Interview commencing at approximately nineteen-hundred hours, with Detectives Nick Hardy and Martha Willis. Suspect being interviewed is Kevin Linn, along with his lawyer Pete Stewart. For the purpose of the tape, I am showing Kevin evidence bag number 8. Kevin, can you confirm the item you are currently looking at?" Nick began.

"A pair of lady's underwear."

"Who do they belong to?" Martha asked.

Kevin looked at his lawyer who shook his head. "No comment." He replied.

"DNA evidence shows that this piece of underwear belonged to our victim, Lisa Marsh. How did you come into possession of them?"

"No comment."

"For the purpose of the tape, I am now showing Kevin images taken of his apartment. Why do you have over 250 obscure pictures of Lisa?"

"Because she is beautiful," Kevin answered. A sigh escaped his lawyers' lips.

"Did you have permission to take these photos?"

"No comment."

"Why were you arguing with the victim the day before she went missing?"

"No comment."

"Where were you on Monday the 9th of January; the night Lisa went missing?" Nick pressed on.

"In my apartment."

"Doing what?"

"Watching TV."

"Alone?"

"Yes."

"So no one can give you an alibi when the kidnapping took place?"

"No comment."

"What were you watching?"

"What the hell has that got to do with this?" Kevin snapped.

"Just answer the question."

Kevin looked to his lawyer who then gave him a nod. "I was watching re-runs of Emmerdale."

"All night?"

"Pretty much."

"So what were you doing when the re-runs finished?"

"I went to bed."

"What time?" Martha asked.

"Gone midnight."

"When was the last time you snorted cocaine?"

"No comment."

"Who would you usually take drugs with?"

"No comment."

"Come on, Kevin. We know you do drugs, and evidence shows more than one person snorting. So who are your druggie friends? Scotty, maybe? Another victim?" Nick spat.

"I'm afraid these questions are going off-topic in regards to Lisa's death, and we have only 2 hours left until you either charge or release my client. And it is becoming apparent to me that you are both grasping at straws, and so I recommend you release Kevin Linn." The lawyer finally spoke up.

"Fine!" Nick forced the word out reluctantly. "He can go. But we'll be watching every move you make. And don't even think about doing a runner, because we will catch you and lock you up, understand?"

"My client and I understand the implications running away could cause." Kevin was silently nodding in agreement with his lawyer.

"Interview suspended at nineteen-hundred-and-forty hours." Martha stopped the tape, and so Kevin was free to walk, leaving the building with his lawyer by his side.

"I've said it before and I'll say it again; son of a fucking bitch!" Nick slammed his fist on the table.

CHAPTER TWELVE

"**So how much longer are you staying at Nick's for?**" Tyler asked. Martha and her best friend were sat in Nick's living room, talking over a cup of tea. Tyler was in her maternity clothes and had a beautiful glow about herself.

"I'm hoping to go back home sometime this week; though I'm still nervous about the fact that there is some creep out there possibly watching my every move. I mean, he knows where I live. He probably knows I'm here right now."

"Bloody hell, hun. Don't be creeping me out too much, my waters might break!" She laughed, rubbing her slowly growing bump.

It had been 3 weeks since the break-in and the arrest of Kevin Linn who managed to lawyer up and go free.

"We'll have officers outside your home undercover at all times." Nick chimed in, settling down in his armchair with a freshly made cup of cocoa coffee.

"I know. But now I just feel like I'm constantly looking over my shoulder." Martha sighed.

"With Nick by your side? You have nothing to worry about. Muscles here will protect you." Tyler winked at them both. Martha tried to hide her face from going red while Nick beamed from ear to ear.

"Don't let your man hear you call me that. We might have to fight over you otherwise," he chirped happily. "So, what have you girls got planned for today?"

"Well, I have treated Tyler to a spa day while I organize a very special baby shower!" Martha's eyes lit up with excitement. Finally, something fun to keep her mind off of the case.

"Honestly, with a baby growing inside me, I cannot wait for this spa!"

"How far gone are you now?" Nick asked.

"17 weeks tomorrow. Which reminds me, I best get going so I don't miss my booking with the spa." Tyler gave her biggest smile. She shared a hug with her best friend, and then with Nick, before heading out of the house and on her way to the land of pure relaxation.

"You sure you up to planning this baby shower?" Nick asked.

"Absolutely. I need something to cheer me up after the past couple of weeks I've had. And there's nothing better than throwing a baby shower for my girl!"

"Well then. You enjoy your day off, and I'll see you later."

"Keep me posted if anything comes up."

"Will do." Grabbing his coat, Nick also left the house, leaving Martha to her own devices.

* * *

It had been a long and tiring day, but Martha had finally finished what she intended: a beautiful baby shower ready to throw in just a few weeks' time. Invitations were made, balloons on order, Nick's permission to hold the party at his place, and catering planned for all the guests as well as some beautiful gifts for mother and baby to be. She had managed to complete all her tasks and it was the best feeling she had experienced for weeks since the break-in.

As Martha finally sat down in the comfy sofa by the fire with a hot cup of tea, Nick walked through the front door. It had just gone 20:38.

"And the man of the house is back!" Martha chirped.

"And I bring with me Scotty's autopsy results." He waved a brown file in one hand while he slid off his coat from the other arm and hung it up.

"Kettle has just boiled. Want a cuppa?"

"I'll have one in a bit. Want to have a look?"

"Of course!" She slapped her hand on the empty seat beside her, prompting Nick to sit down. He opened the file and began to read it aloud.

Scotty Branning, 26 years old, deceased. No previous records or paper trails before the age of 20, identity non-existent. Friends and family non-existent. He is completely off the grid until 2 years ago when he was charged for rape, let off with a caution, community service and £250 fine.

Toxicology report: Overdose on Methadone, 1500mg, a liquid form, resulting in death, believed to be self-inflicted through the left arm due to a fresh needle wound, though the trajectory could prove otherwise. More tests underway.

A black eye, perimortem, believed to be caused by another person, likely to be a mass fight due to further bruising across his body as well as some cracked ribs that had gone untreated. Due to the damage to his body, the attacker must be at least 6ft weighing approximately 88kg.

"What the fuck does it mean by 'non-existent'?" Martha grew confused and slightly annoyed with the results.

"We've looked on all of our databases, ran his ID, photo, prints, nothing. He doesn't exist until the age of 20, and has no police record until his rape case 2 years ago at the age of 24."

"How is that even possible?"

"Either he lived a life off the grid in the middle of London, which, might I add, is virtually impossible. Or, his identity is forged. But if that's the case, why didn't the police pick up on this 2 years ago?"

"Unless it was an inside job, wiping his identity completely and giving him a new one."

"I bloody hope not. This case doesn't need a bad cop added to everything else."

"Tell me about it," Martha sighed. "Well, it has certainly thrown a spanner into the works. How tall do you reckon Kevin Linn is?"

"You thinking Scotty's death could be related to Lisa's death?" Nick began rubbing his chin.

"Well we know Scotty raped her, and now we know his identity is a lie, and he was in a physical fight not too long before OD'ing. I reckon Kevin is due another visit. If he isn't afraid to throw a punch at someone he supposedly loves, imagine his anger if he was to find out Scotty raped her. I believe it's possible that Scotty's death might not have been entirely self-inflicted after all."

"That, or if he can't have her, no one can. We could be looking at a double homicide. We'll get Jessica to re-assess the needle marks to see if it wasn't self-inflicted. This could be big."

CHAPTER THIRTEEN

O nce again, the detectives found themselves back in their office, inundated with work, along with Jessica Heath, head of the Forensic Science Department.

7:03 am. Whiteboard covered with images of the victim along with possible suspects, friends, and family. Scotty's image also occupied the whiteboard.

"Probable causes: accidental overdose. Or..." Nick began.

"Forced upon overdose," Martha added.

"Proof?"

"Examine the trajectory of the needle entry wound. The angle could tell us a whole new story." Jessica interrupted.

"Case notes indicate Scotty was left-handed, but the lethal dose was injected into the left arm." Martha was shifting through Scotty's file.

"Suicide or accidental, why would he inject using his right hand? Unnecessarily awkward and makes no sense. What was the angle of entrance?"

"The needle was injected at a 90-degree angle and penetrated the muscle. This kind of injection is referred to as intramuscular, which also suggests it was not self-inflicted. Somebody else gave Scotty the lethal dose. This was definitely murder. Unfortunately, this was initially missed by one of my ME students which is now under investigation, so thank you for paging me to re-assess the needle puncture site." With

Jessica Heath's final verdict, Martha and Nick knew instantly that this was related to Lisa's murder, but how, and why?

"So who do we know about so far?" Nick asked.

"Jason Stark, our victim's boyfriend. Reported to be abusive toward her, could have been an attack gone wrong. It is also possible he had links with Scotty. Maybe he knew something about our victim resulting in Jason staging a suicide to cover his tracks. Although he has a stable alibi the night of Lisa's death, he has yet to explain why he never reported his girlfriend missing. Maybe because he knew where she was the entire time, what with his track record of physical abuse." Martha explained.

"Then we have Kevin Linn, the victims' mother's carer; beholds a shrine to our victim in his bedroom, CCTV footage of him hitting her, and a confession to possessing illegal drugs which could then tie to the murder of Scotty. His motive being if he can't have her, then no one can."

"Lillian Marsh, our victim's mother. Has Alzheimer's Dementia, is prone to bouts of anger and aggression, and could have attacked her daughter in a fit of rage, completely out of her control. This could have encouraged Lisa to run away, what with the stress and anger her mum could have caused, resulting in her getting kidnapped. This literally could be a simple case of 'wrong place at the wrong time.'"

"I would say the mother is innocent. The abuse Lisa was subjected to was too severe to be caused by a frail old lady, in addition to the rapes she suffered. Forensics shows she was subjected to more rapes than just the two that took place perimortem." Jessica interjected.

"Kevin's looking more and more suspect the longer we investigate him. What killed Scotty *exactly*?" Nick asked.

"He was injected with 1500mg of methadone, which is a synthetic opioid. Whoever it belonged to, they would have paid at least £3000 to be able to get their hands on liquid meth."

"I think our best option is to figure out whom the meth belonged to, and who injected it into Scotty. I feel if we find that out, it will bring us one step closer to finding the identity of Lisa Marsh's killer." Martha concluded.

"Anyone else we haven't mentioned?" Nick asked.

"We have Olivier Carmen, Jason Starks alibi. She confirmed to have been with him the night of Lisa's murder, so that rules him out. That, or they were both in it together, given his abusive lifestyle. And as mentioned, he never reported Lisa missing. In addition to treating Scotty's death as suspicious, I believe we should meet with Olivier Carmen and get the full story of her involvement with our victim's boyfriend. I still can't get past the fact that no one other than her mother reported her missing. If more people came forward, it would have pressured the Missing Persons team to move forward with the case, but no one did, not her boyfriend, her stalker, her boss, or even any friends? I'd like to try and track down more people who were close to Lisa and find out exactly why they had no concerns for her safety for the two weeks she was held missing for. I can't imagine the fear and pain she endured, hoping someone would find her, but no one came forward except a dementia patient. They probably assumed it was all in her head. We literally had no chance of saving her."

"Finally we have Leanne Baker, the woman who found Lisa's body. She was on her way back home from work when she stumbled across the scene. Unfortunately, Lisa was already deceased upon discovery." Jessica concluded.

"Right, we track down the person who is dealing liquid meth, find out who his customers are, hopefully, get a solid lead on the murder of Scotty Branning. In addition to this, we track down some of Lisa's friends, find out what is going on there and if they know anything that could help with our investigation. Another visit to Kevin may be on the cards, too, and I would like to meet with Leanne Baker again. Everyone happy with the plan of action?" Martha and Jessica nodded in agreement with Nick's plan, and so the meeting came to a tidy close.

* * *

Martha Willis and Nick Hardy pulled up in his Mazda outside of Leanne Bakers home just as his phone began to ring. "Hey Michael, what you got for me?" Michael Lance, Computer Analysis Expert. "Cheers, I'll let Martha know. Thanks, mate." He put the phone down.

"News?"

"Indeed. The day before Lisa's disappearance, she bought herself a one-way ticket to Australia, ready to depart the next morning. A digital receipt was found amongst her emails, along with a very detailed Facebook message sent to her boyfriend, Jason, explaining how she can't be with him anymore and that she needs to get away from him and her mum. Now that is a motive if I'd ever seen one."

"That is definitely a biggie. And it begs the question, why hasn't Jason told us this himself?"

"We'll interview Leanne and as soon as we're done we're going straight to his. Hopefully he's home." The two detectives left the car with fresh information brewing around lively in their minds and rang on Leanne's doorbell.

"Hello?" Leanne opened the door just a crack and peered out.

"Hi, Leanne Baker, it's Detective Willis and my partner Detective Hardy. We're here about the body you found, you said we could visit any time if we had any questions."

"Oh, yes, of course, come in." She opened the door further and gestured for the detectives to go through to the living room, all whilst rubbing her left ear that was covered with a Band-Aid. The house in general was well lit with a light grey and white theme throughout. "Please, have a seat," she offered as she sat in the armchair, leaving the detectives to find comfort in the 3-seater sofa. "I'm afraid I cannot offer much help as I have already told you everything I knew on the day, but I will do my best to assist."

"That's absolutely fine, thank you. It's just to go over what we have already discussed and confirmed that we're not missing out any details." Nick assured her. "Would you be able to tell us exactly what happened that morning?"

"Well, I was on my way home from work at about 6 am. I work night shifts, you see. It usually takes half an hour to get home but I missed my bus so had to walk, which makes it an hour journey. Where I found the poor woman, I was only 15 minutes away from home. It was awful. I thought it was a dummy at first. A nasty joke, you know? But when I got closer I saw she was real, that the blood was real. I don't even want to begin to imagine what was done to her."

"How do you mean?" Martha asked.

"Well there must have been a sexual assault because she was un-clothed. It was definitely men that did this."

"Men? Plural?" Nick pressed.

"Well, maybe not 'men', but definitely male. I doubt a woman could cause so much damage to one person, and if she was raped, it was a man, don't you think?"

"I can see your logic, Miss Baker. Although it is possible for a woman to rape someone, though the statistics are lower than the actual numbers. Just for future reference." Martha intersected. *Professional? I don't know, but she needs to know the truth, no matter how hard it may be. Maybe not the right time or place though. Keep it together,* she thought.

"Yes, of course. I'm sorry."

"It's fine. This is a hard case for all of us." *Nick saving the day again. Bless him and his caring heart.* "How did the scene look before we arrived.

79

Any clothing you may have noticed?"

"No, I'm sorry. It looked exactly how you found it yourself. I refused to touch anything, you know, in case I messed up the crime scene, like in the TV shows and stuff."

"Yes. Was there anything you may have forgotten to tell us at the time that you could inform us of today?"

"Hm, I don't think so. I'm so sorry, I want to be of more help but I really don't know anything else. I'm sorry." Her eyes began to tear up.

"No, Miss Baker, it's absolutely fine. We're sorry to bring this back to your door. We'll let you get on with the rest of your day." Martha said sympathetically, and both the detectives left the house.

"Nothing new as of yet," Nick said, climbing back into the driver's seat.

"So, mother or boyfriend next?"

"Boyfriend. That Jason has something to hide and I'm going to find out exactly what it is!" He thrust the gear in place and pulled the car away aggressively. The time spent on this case started to feel as though it was closing in on the detectives. Something had to give.

CHAPTER FOURTEEN

"**Jason Stark, it's Detective Hardy and Detective Willis from the MSMI, open up!**" Nick banged on his front door belligerently.

"Yes, yes, okay!" He yelled from within. Upon opening the door he was tying up the belt to his black knee-length dressing-gown. "Do you mind? I have a guest and you're intruding!"

"Not intruding at all, Jason. We just need to ask you a few more questions. Who's your guest?"

"Is that one of your questions?"

"It is now and I'll arrest you for obstructing the law if you don't fucking answer!"

"Jesus fucking Christ! It's just some girl I met at the fucking bar, man!"

"Just 'some girl'? Are you fucking serious?" A young, blonde woman was stood just behind him, wearing nothing but a white bath towel. "What the fuck Jason! I'm getting dressed and I'm leaving!" She yelled, storming back into the bedroom she had just come from.

"I didn't mean it like that! For fuck sake man! You coppers ruin everything. Fucking dicks!"

"Sorry to ruin your grieving over your not-long-deceased girlfriend, but I can see you're handling it very well." Nick pressed.

"I swear to god you say one more fucking word and I will fucking deck you!"

"Go on. See where hitting an officer will get you, I dare you!"

"Nick, no!" Martha gasped, but it was too late. A loud thud and Nick's lip cut instantly.

Nick grabbed hold of Jason, turned him around, and shoved him up against the wall. "Jason Stark, I'm arresting you for assaulting an officer of the law. You do not have to say anything, but it may harm your defence if you do not mention when questioned something which you may later rely on in court. Anything you do say may be given in evidence. I've been waiting to do this since the day we met!" Nick placed a half-naked Jason in handcuffs and forced him out of his flat and straight into the back of his car. Just from the look of his face, Martha could tell Nick was enjoying every moment of arresting this abusive arsehole.

* * *

Jason found himself sitting in a warm interrogation room within the MSMI Department. The room was sophisticated and well-lit, but with black walls and grey carpet. Martha and Nick were sat opposite the metal table Jason was at, a file with his name on just in front of them, open on a page full of his past convictions, and the tape machine was sat at the end of the table recording everything.

"Not a very innocent person, are you, Mr Stark?"

"You know fuck all 'bout me, Detective Hardy!" He snapped back at him.

"Well, I know you're not leaving this place any time soon. I also know you will be spending a few nights in a cell for hitting me. And, I also know that you've been perverting the course of justice by keeping things hidden from our investigation!"

"I've been perverting nothing!"

"Oh really? So you don't know anything about your recently murdered girlfriend's plans to run away and move countries?" Martha stepped in quite happily.

"How the fuck do you know that?"

"It doesn't take a genius to look through a victim's Facebook messages, but we had one do so anyway, and boy are you in some deep shit!" Nick was revelling in the beauty of this interrogation. He pulled out a piece of paper from another file that was under Jason's, this file being Lisa's murder investigation. "For the purpose of the tape, I will now read from evidence number 6.9. "*Jason, I can't do this anymore*'," he began to read. "'*I can't stand any more bruises, broken bones, lying to my friends. I hurt, and I know I have done nothing to deserve this treatment. You call me names, you throw me around. I have enough of my own mother hurting me, but at least it isn't her fault. I just can't take this pain anymore. I'm running away, and there is nothing you can do to stop me. I'm not telling you where I am going, but just know I have always loved you, even with everything you have ever put me through. I'm sorry. Goodbye.*' Hmm, sounds like you were losing your punching bag, aye."

"Little slag didn't have it in her! I didn't tell you 'bout that message cause bitch was goin' nowhere!"

"Well, why did she have a one-way ticket to Australia? No return." Martha slid a picture of the plane tickets across the table to him.

"Nah, she was just foolin'. You fuckers know nothing!"

"Well we know you have a history of abusing our victim, said so in her own words, and the day after our victim broke up with your abusive arse, she ends up going missing; two weeks later she is found dead. Now, I don't know about you, but to me that rings motive, and you most certainly had the opportunity, what with her Facebook message warning you exactly what she was about to do, you had time to stop her."

"And do you have any evidence to back that up? Because I could sue your arse for slander!" Jason was clenching his teeth, his face bright red with anger.

"Not yet, but we will."

"Well good luck with that, because you can't get evidence of something that never happened!"

"Maybe not, but I hope you enjoy your next few nights in a nice cold prison cell!" Nick slammed his hands on the table as he stood, turned off the tape machine and left the room.

"If you know anything about your girlfriends' murder, you better come forward and say it now, because otherwise, things are only going to get worse." Martha pleaded, but the response was a silent stare, and so she too left the interrogation room.

"I don't think he'll be spilling beans any time soon" Martha sighed to Nick.

"At least we got him locked up, for now, save him from screwing with any more women in the meantime."

"So what's next?"

"Well, thanks to Michael Lance and his skills with computing, we now have two friends of interest who have agreed to meet with us. He messaged me their names and address about an hour ago."

"Ah, the power of Facebook, huh?"

"Indeed, the power of Facebook. Ready?"

"Ready." And on that note, the detectives left the MSMI Bureau.

* * *

"Melanie Kartwright and Hazel Brent?" Martha asked as the two girls answered the door together. "I'm Detective Martha Willis and this is my partner, Detective Nick Hardy."

"Yes, we were expecting you. Please, c-come in." Hazel stuttered. The 4 of them walked into the dining room and sat around the marble-topped table.

"We have it to believe you're both friends of Lisa Marsh?" Nick asked gently.

"Yes. We've been friends since high school. Year 9 I think." Melanie answered with a smile.

"When was the last time you saw Lisa?"

"It was before C-C-Christmas," Hazel remembered. "We were planning a new year party together, b-but she never showed up."

"We messaged her on Facebook asking if she was okay, why she didn't turn up. She said she couldn't talk, and then blocked us both. After that, we didn't see her again until it was announced on the news that her body was found." Melanie's voice broke as she spoke of her friend's early demise. Hazel reached for her hand and they comforted each other simultaneously.

"Do you know why she couldn't talk and why she couldn't make it to the party?" Martha was writing notes in her flipbook.

"No, b-but we have a pretty good idea that it was b-because of her b-boyfriend, Jason."

"What makes you believe it was because of him?"

"He always stopped her from hanging out with us. And she was pretty open about him hurting her. We kept telling her to dump the shit-head but she wouldn't. She was constantly making excuses for him, blaming herself, that she deserved it. Your typical abused girlfriend. Nothing we said would take her away from him. We didn't even realise Lisa was missing otherwise we would have reported it. We would have reported the abuse but she swore us to secrecy. We were hoping that soon enough she would realise what he was doing, unblock us on Facebook and find a safe haven in her besties. It was only when we saw her picture on the news that we blamed ourselves for her death because we weren't there for her; we just left her in the arms of that creep."

"Did he—Did he kill her?" Hazel choked on the words.

"We don't know. At the moment we are trying to rule people out. Do you know a Scotty Branning?"

"Yeah. I had a fling with him once. He was almost as shitty as Jason, except he never hit me. It was all just words instead." Melanie was clearly angry over her memories with him. "Don't tell me he had something to do with Lisa's death?"

"Unfortunately yes. He raped her shortly before she died." Nick said sternly.

"What?!" The girls screeched at the same time.

"That disgusting, perverted shit-face! Have you arrested him? That fucking cunt!" Melanie's fury was gut-wrenching.

"No, we haven't arrested him. He's dead."

"What? How?"

"An overdose."

"Fucking druggie cunt! So he got away with murder?"

"Not entirely. We believe his overdose wasn't self-inflicted."

"So he raped and murdered Lisa, and then someone murdered him?" She was crying now.

"We're not entirely sure exactly what has happened, or that he was Lisa's direct murderer, but we're working on it and we will find out what happened and bring justice to Lisa," Martha explained as kindly as she could. The interview was drawn to a close and proved to be somewhat useful for the detectives.

* * *

The day was coming to an end as the sun set over London. The sky had turned a pinky-purple colour, and the snow that once encapsulated the city was finally melting away, though great amounts of ice and slush remained. Martha found herself back in Nick's apartment, dressed in cosy pyjamas and having a cup of hot chocolate-flavoured Horlicks. Nick had joined her for this evening routine and the partners spoke briefly about the day they had just had and where it was leading the investigation.

"Jason is looking like one of our top suspects, but with an alibi up his sleeve, there's nothing we can do. And he will be out soon enough after punching me."

"Honestly don't know how you refrained yourself from beating the shit out of him," Martha giggled slightly.

"Oh, it was difficult but so worth it, getting him in cuffs like he deserves. This case won't be successful until that dickhead is behind bars for life."

"I think we should give his alibi a visit, see what went down between them. She may have been his alibi for the murder, but we have yet to confirm his whereabouts the morning Lisa was kidnapped. If she was just a one night stand, then she wasn't around for the entire two weeks that Lisa was missing. Jason could have been doing anything in that time."

"Like forcing a brutal attack on his poor victim. All those bruises and broken bones. She had suffered a great deal before her life was snatched away." Nick took the last sip from his mug and set it down on the coffee table. "Plans for tomorrow?"

"Talk to Jason's alibi in person, and re-interview him, see what he was doing for two weeks that completely over-rode the importance of his own girlfriends' disappearance."

"I can most certainly agree with that." And so the evening was over and the tired detectives said their goodnights and went to their rooms, calling it a night.

CHAPTER FIFTEEN

Martha and Nick made their way to Olivier Carmen's home ready to talk to her about the alibi she had given Jason Stark. She lived in a rented bungalow with her dog Bunny, a very loud Chihuahua that wouldn't stop yapping at the detectives.

"I'm sorry about her; she gets very protective of me when new people come to visit." She led Bunny into the back garden and shut the door behind her, enabling the detectives and herself to take a seat in the confined but cosy living room.

"Did you know Jason had a girlfriend when you slept together?" Nick asked.

"Not at all. If I had known, I would never have gone home with him. I feel awful about everything that has happened, and it makes my skin crawl knowing what I did while his girlfriend was facing the most terrifying moment of her entire life." She began to hold back tears, trying to stay strong and collected. "I haven't slept since I found out what happened. All I can see in my dreams is what Jason and I did, and then his poor girlfriend getting attacked. It's awful, it's sick!"

"It wasn't your fault, though. Remember that." Martha consoled.

"How did it happen?" asked Nick.

"What, you mean how did we meet and end up having sex? We were in a nightclub, we got drunk, and one thing led to another. Your basic night out story that makes me sound like your common slag. I'm not

88

happy about it, and to be honest, I would have preferred it if no one knew about it, but knowing Jason was facing kidnapping charges for the night he was with me? I couldn't sit by and lie and let someone go down for a crime they didn't commit just to save myself from looking like a whore."

"So he had no involvement in Lisa's kidnapping?" Nick pushed on.

"As far as I am aware, no, he had no involvement. He was still at his place when I left about midday the next day. The ultimate walk of shame. And then two weeks later I find out not only did he have my phone number, but he also had a girlfriend who ended up kidnapped and then murdered. Honestly, this is the most awful thing I have ever been involved in. To be honest, I'm not coping that well."

"We can get you numbers for the crisis teams and MIND if needed?" Martha offered.

"MIND?"

"Yes. They are a charity that helps with mental health and difficult situations, to offer support and help you cope."

"That would be great if you could! I think it may do me some good." With her confirmation, Martha ripped a page out from her notebook and wrote down the contact numbers and emails for MIND, and then handed it over to Olivier who was so grateful that she hugged Martha.

"You have been a great help, Olivier. Thank you!" Nick said with a reassuring smile.

After calming Olivier down, the detectives eventually left her bungalow and headed back to their office in the MSMI Bureau.

CHAPTER SIXTEEN

I t was now 32 days since the investigation into Lisa's death had begun, yet it felt like a lifetime. Martha found herself waking up to the sound of her phone ringing. Jessica Heath, Forensic Anthropologist.

"Hey, what you got for me?"

"I am afraid that those cigarette butts from the parking lot at your apartment have led us to a dead end. No matches were made. I am sorry. We will still be working on finding any evidence that can lead us at least one step closer to the man who broke into your home."

"Thank you, it means a lot having such a great support network. Shame about the fags. Thank you again."

"No problem. Give me a call if and when you need. Any new leads on Lisa's case?"

"Unfortunately not yet. I feel like we're stuck in a loop, but her boyfriend and stalker are looking rather suspicious. Who knows nowadays. Anyone seems capable of anything. I'll let you get back to your work. Thanks again."

"See you later!"

The phone call left Martha feeling a little disheartened, what with being no closer to catching the perpetrator who broke into her home and left the threatening note. *Soon, we will get him soon!* She chanted to herself.

"Everything okay?" Nick asked after knocking on the door of her temporary room, stepping inside cautiously.

"Yeah, it was just Jessica. They couldn't find any matches for the cigarette butts."

"Sorry to hear."

"Nah, it's fine. If they did find a match it would still be highly unlikely that it was from the man who broke into my apartment. It's been 3 weeks since the break-in and no one has heard or seen anything since, so I think I'll go home tonight after work."

"Only if you're sure?"

"Yeah, I think it's been long enough."

"Would you like me to stay round for the night, so you can get settled?" He was now sat at the end of Martha's bed.

"Nah. I'll be okay."

"You sure?"

"Promise. Now let's get up and ready for work, we have a murder to solve."

"Aye-aye captain," he said, saluting her as he stood up.

* * *

Martha had just put the phone down after a lengthy conversation with their boss, Mohammad Muskhan, all while Nick drove them to the nearest McDonalds for breakfast. "They've let Jason go. They've charged him for assaulting you: 62 hours of community service and a £5000 fine."

"Well, at least it's something, even if the little shit deserves a lot more. We'll get him."

"That's not all. His alibi for both the night Lisa was murdered and the morning her body was found checks out. He was at his local the entire time, passed out by the bar after drinking one too many. Looks like he isn't our killer. Also, no match for his DNA against the swab of sperm that was taken, so he isn't our rapist either. And before I forget, forensics checked his place, no knife, so it's looking like he didn't assault her this time around. That or he has successfully disposed of the weapon."

"So you're telling me that fucked up, druggie little cunt could actually be innocent?" Nick was clearly fuming by this point, his face a dark red with pure anger.

"So far, yes. But we do have some good news! Jason has given us the name of the drug dealer who dealt the Liquid Meth that ended up killing Scotty. His name is Zahid Maul, but Jason still denies involvement and has a solid alibi so he couldn't have killed Scotty, either. Another night at the pub, apparently. Oh, and it turns out that the semen samples that were destroyed was an accident caused by Taz. Apparently, she has been in tears to her dad all morning. He believes her, of course, so no action is taking place. But at least we managed to re-test the remaining semen before she ruined anything else."

"Fucking hell! At least we're finally getting somewhere! Still not happy about Jason being free to roam the streets, though."

"Tell me about it. I'm still convinced he was involved somehow. I can just feel it in my gut."

"Then we will go by your gut feeling because I'm pretty fucking certain he did something to that poor girl in the time she was missing, and we're going to find out exactly what, where, and why. In the meantime, let's check up on Lillian Marsh, see if she has remembered anything new, then we'll try and find this drug dealer."

* * *

"We are so sorry, Miss Marsh." Martha was practically begging for forgiveness.

"No! You're nothing but liars!"

Martha and Nick had spent the last two hours with Lisa's mother, Lillian Marsh. Since their last visit, her condition seemed to have deteriorated; she forgot about her daughter's disappearance and her murder. When reporting this back to the team at the MSMI Bureau, Jessica confirmed that the grief of losing her daughter may have exacerbated the Alzheimer's Dementia, leaving her in denial of what had happened. The visit ended with Lillian screaming and swearing, taking everything out on the detectives who were clueless on how to calm an Alzheimer's patient.

"Where's Kevin?" Martha asked Lillian as politely as possible.

"Who's Kevin! And who are you? To come in here and tell me my daughter is dead? You're sick! Both of you are sick!" She screamed, tears streaming down her face. The entire episode proved difficult for the detectives; it was heart-wrenching seeing someone suffer in such an awful way, literally at war with their own mind, nothing making sense.

"We're very sorry, Mrs Marsh. We are so sorry to come in here and upset you." Nick explained.

"Get out! I want you both out!" She began marching them to her front door and physically pushed them through. "I said, GET OUT!"

* * *

Martha and Nick were once again in the car, a new habit since the beginning of the case.

"Are you okay?" He asked gently.

"Yeah, I've just never seen anything like that before. It was awful. That poor woman. She thinks Lisa is still alive. It breaks my heart." A single tear travelled slowly from her left eye, down her rosy cheeks, and eventually fell from her jawline.

"I know. It was pretty scary to be fair. I mean, what do we do? Usually we keep family members in the loop of a case involving their loved ones, but it seems this will only aggravate the situation and make Lillian's condition worse."

"I think it's best we phone social services. Kevin doesn't seem to be around 24/7, and I think it's clear to say Lillian needs that now. And from now on, we may have to go through social rather than her when we have any updates on the case."

"I think you're right. She can't go on like that. She doesn't look like she's been eating properly, either. She looks almost skeletal."

Upon mutual agreement, Martha decided it was time to phone social services before moving on to tracking down Zahid Maul.

CHAPTER SEVENTEEN

Martha and Nick found themselves under a run down, un-used bridge where a group of homeless drug addicts had set up camp. The snow had melted leaving the ground soaked in water and slush, proving to be very slippery under the detective's feet. The temperature was reaching -2, and so the homeless people were all dressed in ripped coats and jackets, and some were wrapped in rough grey blankets that had been donated to them via charities.

"Can't remember the last time I visited a homeless camp," Martha said glumly, with a hint of guilt.

"You reckon we're in the right place?" Nick asked while blowing into his hands, trying to keep himself warm.

"Michael has heard of Zahid and apparently he has quite a presence online, advertising that he deals at homeless shelters on certain days. He's supposed to be due here today according to his accounts."

"How have the police not arrested him if he is clearly advertising illegal activities?"

"I wish I had the answer to that."

"Slacking, that's why!"

"Well, he won't be free for much longer. We just have to keep our eyes open for him."

The detectives took a seat on a public bench just a few feet away from the main group of homeless people, knowing that where a crowd forms, Zahid would be likely to make an appearance.

A few hours had passed since Martha and Nick began their surveillance at the nearby bench. Every other hour they would take in turns buying themselves hot chocolate and coffee from the nearest Starbucks, just 5 minutes away, in order to keep themselves warm and hydrated in the bitterly cold conditions they found themselves in. On the 6th hour, a crowd began to form. Zahid was there. The detectives spied him in an instant due to his Nike Brand tracksuit, standing out from all the homeless wearing their tattered clothes. They began walking towards him, throwing the last of their hot drinks into the nearest bin. As the crowd turned and saw them, they slowly began parting, like waves, creating a human-guided pathway directly toward Zahid himself.

"Ah, two new customers I see, how can I be of help?" He asked bravely.

"MSMI," Jason revealed his badge to him. "We need a word about Jason Stark and Scotty Branning."

"Detectives, huh? Come to shut me down?"

"Not really our job, but we can and we will if you don't cooperate," Martha pressed.

"Fair dos, fair dos." He paused a minute and then gestured for the crowd to disperse and leave them to talk in private. Being their drug dealer - their 'God' - the crowd obeyed and were gone in seconds. "So, how can I help?"

"Jason Stark's girlfriend was found raped and murdered. Scotty Branning, one of the last people to have seen her alive, was also found dead."

"Yes, I saw on the news. An overdose?"

"Yes, but not self-inflicted," Nick replied.

"Ah, 2 murders and Jason Stark is in the middle of them both. Interesting. What about the rest of his gang?"

"Gang? What gang?" Nick barked.

"Oh, you don't know, do you? Jason has a nifty little gang, if I may say so."

"They could be involved in Lisa's murder," Martha said to Nick.

"What are their names?" Nick ordered Zahid to cough up.

"And why should I offer that kind of information, and risk my life in doing so?"

"Jason played ball and offered you up as his and Scotty's dealer, and your online presence backs this up. You could be looking at years in prison."

"Well then, if he wants to play ball, I'm willing to confess if I keep my freedom."

"We can't promise that." Nick huffed.

"Well, what exactly do you want to know?"

"Did you deal Jason liquid meth?"

"Ah, yes. That was a big purchase indeed."

"How did you get hold of such a large quantity?"

"A magician never shares his secrets!"

"Well, that purchase resulted in Scotty's overdose, meaning you could be facing manslaughter charges!" Nick sighed heavily.

"No, I can't go down for that!"

"How long have you known Jason and Scotty for?" Martha asked.

"Years, more than 10 at least. Why?"

"I'm willing to cut you a deal, reduce the chances, or at least the sentence, of you going down for manslaughter."

"What do you need?"

"Will you be willing to give up the identities of Jason's gang members? That's the only deal we are willing to make. Their names for your freedom."

"Okay. There is 6 of them altogether, including Jason himself and Scotty."

"If you can give us their names and contact details, we will cut you the deal. And we won't tell them you snitched, either, so you don't have to worry about going into hiding."

"Hm, I guess I could do that."

"Cough up, then!" Nick said, impatient, mostly due to the intensely cold air and the fresh snowflakes that began to fall.

"Okay, okay. Take a chill pill, mate. We have Royce Arnold, Shawn Rose, Keegan Lloyd, and Clyde Bennet."

"Do you know where we can find them?"

"I do indeed."

"Are you willing to corroborate this back at the MSMI Bureau? Sign a contract confirming the deal?"

"If it lessens my punishment for involuntary involvement then we have a deal." Zahid smiled at the detectives, causing Nick to roll his eyes.

Martha led the way back to Nick's Mazda and got in, welcomed with the warmth of the heater that Nick had left on, ready for their journey back to work.

* * *

"So we officially have their names and addresses, meaning we can interview them all and take swabs to test their involvement in the rapes that Lisa endured. We also know where Jason got the liquid meth that killed Scotty, but he still denies being involved. With Zahid's voluntary confessions, we may be able to get Jason to talk, but I'm not holding my breath for that." Martha let out a deep sigh. *How can we get him to talk when he is so damn fucking stubborn?* She thought.

"We'll get him eventually, as more things start to pile up against him.

In the meantime, we need to make sure we have explored all avenues and confirm we're not missing anything detrimental to the case."

CHAPTER EIGHTEEN

"**Who, what, when, where, why, and how!**" Nick barked at himself. The two detectives were back in their office along with Jessica Heath; the forensic anthropologist, David Mace; the DNA research and analysis guru, so they called him, and Michael Lance; computer analysis expert.

"Lisa was kidnapped and held captive for two weeks, before being raped multiple times and then murdered. Who did it is unknown." Jessica Heath was sat on the right side of the long, 8-seated-table that took up most of the room of the group office. The whiteboards that covered one of the walls were mostly covered in pictures and writing relating to the case, and anything stated in this meeting was being added to the boards by Nick Hardy himself.

"The kidnapping took place on the 9th of January 2017, when Lisa was taken on her way to work. No witnesses have come up as of yet. She was found unclothed in the back of an ally. Where she was being kept for the two weeks of her disappearance is also yet to be discovered," Martha explained.

"Any leads on where she may have been kept, David?" Nick asked.

"I'm currently running multiple tests on any kind of particulates found on Lisa's body and the surrounding area of where she was found in order to determine the type of place she was held hostage. It's looking like she was being held in some kind of warehouse due to some of the results, but it is still inconclusive. I suggest, at this point, to start a search on abandoned warehouses around the place her body was found. If I could take samples of these warehouses and match any of the particulates, then we will have the whereabouts that she was being held against her will."

"So we know *what* happened, *when* it happened, almost have *where* it happened, and *how* it happened, and where the liquid meth came from, as well as the names and addresses of Jason's gang members, but we still don't know *who* did it, and *why* they did it. We have one suspect whose DNA was found on the body, but he was murdered shortly after Lisa's demise, and it was made to look like an overdose. Whoever killed Scotty has to be our second murderer slash rapist. Two killers, one dead, one on the run. Who is it, and why did they do it?" Nick was clearly wracking his brains about the case, but he was getting nowhere closer to the answer. "Is there anything else on her computer that can help us build this case?"

"Unfortunately not. Other than her plans of running away and the message sent to Jason, nothing on her computer gives away what happened when she was taken, or any hints on who it could have been." Michael looked tired, heavy dark bags beneath his bloodshot eyes.

Too much time on the computer, maybe? Martha thought to herself.

"Right, we need a plan of action. Martha and I are going to visit Kevin once more. Jessica, I want you to work with David to try and match any particulates that could narrow down what type of warehouse Lisa was being held in, and whereabouts in London that would be. Look close to the scene of the crime, there's no way she could have run far through London without clothes and no one witnessing this. Michael, keep digging through her computer if you still have no luck don't worry. Martha and I will be applying for a warrant to take Kevin's computer away, and we will need you bright-eyed and bushy-tailed for this job, got it?"

"Got it!" Michael said with a smile, possibly relieved that he will finally have something else to look at rather than the same computer he has done for the past couple of weeks.

Damn, he is so fit when he takes charge, Martha's mind, running away with thoughts on her partner yet again. *Pack it in, girl. Stay professional.*

* * *

Kevin's apartment once again; this time he was home, and this time he let the detectives in without so much of a fuss.

"Look, if you've come to arrest me again, I swear I haven't done anything."

"We would like to take your computer," Martha said.

"You what? Why?" Kevin began raising his voice.

"We have a warrant that says we can take it for analysis." Martha waved the piece of paper in the air, under Kevin's nose.

"And what exactly are you hoping to find on there?"

"Well, for your sake, I hope we don't find anything incriminating at all, although something tells me you will probably have more images of Lisa without her knowledge and permission, so you'd be facing charges for that." Nick barked.

"What? Why?"

"Because it's stalking, Kevin, and stalking is illegal; it has been since 2012 under the Protection from Harassment Act. Want to fight that? Then fight it in court!" Martha was riled up by this point. She just couldn't understand how someone like Kevin was able to walk free despite having a shrine of their victim all over his bedroom wall.

Michael Lance from the Computer Analysis Department entered Kevin's apartment with a large container ready to pack Kevin's laptop and computer away. "This should only take a couple of minutes."

"That's fine, thank you." Nick replied peacefully, finally getting somewhere in regards to Kevin's possible involvement in the case.

"I want that computer back in one piece!" Kevin yelled to Michael, forcing his chest out to look big and aggressive.

Nick was having none of it and instantly pushed him back. "Easy there. We don't want to be arresting you again now, do we? In fact, how's that broken wrist of yours?" He said mockingly. Kevin instantly backed down and allowed them all to do the jobs they came to do. "And, before we go, how come you're not at Lillian Marsh's house looking after her?"

"Simple, innit. I quit. I was only looking after her so Lisa and I could be together, now she is dead I have no reason to be in that house."

"You have every reason to be in that house! That poor woman is supposed to be in your care, and right now she is upset, terrified and alone!" Martha snapped.

"Not my problem. I told social she's someone else's problem now, and there's nothing you can do about it. Now hurry up and get out of my gaff."

* * *

"So, what have we got?" Nick asked. The two detectives were in the computer analysis lab within the MSMI Bureau with Michael Lance. It had been an entire 24 hours since confiscating the computer from Kevin.

"Porn. Lots of porn. And I mean . . . more porn than I have ever seen in my lifetime."

"Anything relating to the case?" Martha's best efforts of changing the subject from porn.

"Well, Nick, you were right about the images of our victim, most of which were taken without her consent."

"How can you tell?"

"For a start, the images have been taken from across the street looking into her bedroom window all the while she is getting undressed."

"Son of a bitch!" Nick fumed.

"Can we get him charged for stalking without a live victim to testify?" Martha pondered.

"Well, we can certainly try. His lawyer will have a field day trying to talk their way out of this one."

"Anything else?"

"Not yet. I'll page you if I find anything of use to our case."

"Thanks, mate," Nick grabbed hold of Michael's shoulder and squeezed, the manly equivalent of a hug. "Appreciate it."

"Oh, hang on a second. Just found this . . ." Michael gestured to the computer screen.

"A one way ticket to Australia," Martha read aloud.

"Son of a bitch was going to follow her across the world!" Nick said in disbelief.

"Not just that, listen to this:

"*You can't run away from me forever, for we are meant to be together. Love knows no boundaries where I am from, and if you keep rejecting me, it will make you more glum. My love for you will never die, so please can we stop living in this lie. Let us be the item we should, for I am certain that we could. Please stop pushing me away, as by your side is where I should lay. If you push me aside one last time, I'm afraid I will have to burn your shrine. As all copies of your face burn, I will make sure that it's finally your turn. For what? You may say, and I answer, for this will be your last day.*"

"A poem, a death threat in a fucking poem!" Martha fumed.

"That is sick. We hit the nail on the head when we said if he can't have her then no one can."

"We're bringing him in. Bitch better kiss the light of day goodbye."

* * *

Detectives Nick Hardy and Martha Willis found themselves heading toward the interrogation room in which Kevin was once again waiting, along with his lawyer who had probably already told his client to say "no comment" to all the questions that were going to be fired his way.

Just before opening the door, they were stopped in their tracks.

"Martha, Nick!" A timid voice called out. They turned to where the voice came from and was confronted with a police officer who was fiddling with his hands. "I hear you're working on a case involving a Scotty Branning?"

"Yeah, why?" Martha asked.

"There's someone on the phone wanting to speak with you both. He's on speaker in interrogation room 4. Are you free? He says it is urgent."

"Yeah, sure. Make our suspect sweat a bit more." Nick chirped.

* * *

Another warm, confined room. Martha and Nick sat opposite each other with the phone between them on speaker. An ex-officer, Karl Wright, was on the other end. Martha and Nick stared at each other, intrigued by what this could possibly be about.

"Can we just confirm that this is off the record?" The officer asked.

"Why?" Nick pushed.

"Because if they find out I grassed my family will be killed."

"They? Who's they?" Martha asked, confused.

"I just need to trust you both to keep this quiet. I am putting my life at risk in order to help with your investigation, but if they find out I blabbed then my family will be killed, and then so will I."

"Sounds like you're in some serious shit here, Officer Wright."

"Please, I just need to know I can trust you before I put everything on the line." His voice was trembling badly, clearly through fear.

"Okay, we promise. But we also promise to keep you and your family safe. Now, what is it about Scotty and our case that is so detrimental to you and your family's safety?"

CHAPTER NINETEEN

"It was a few years ago. 7, I think. There was a serial rapist on the loose and the police force was being pounded by the media. 6 women had been raped in the space of 3 months. It was hell. No one could catch a break what with our superiors breathing down our necks day in, day out, threatening to sack us if we didn't find the culprit. They were dark times, and slowly the public started losing hope in us. We ended up arresting a handful of vigilantes who tried to take on the job themselves, but that just resulted in many innocent men being beaten and left for dead while the real serial rapist was left to roam undetected. We found ourselves hospitalising innocent men and arresting groups of 'innocent' gangs for trying to take the law into their own hands.

"Anyhow, one day while patrolling the streets, I caught him in the act. The day was coming to an end and so the streets were barely lit by the street lamps. I was walking past a small alley when I heard shuffling and murmurs. I went to investigate and that's when I saw him, Scotty Branning, raping a drugged-up woman who could barely string a sentence together or hold herself up. I suspected he'd drugged her, but at the time *he* wasn't Scotty Branning, but a Scot Guilds."

"So Scotty Branning is a made up identity?" Martha interrupted.

"Yes."

"That explains why he was seen as off the grid with no history at all," Nick concluded.

"Indeed."

"How did he get a new identity if you caught him in the act?"

"I'll get to that shortly. Please, patience.

"I jumped on top of him and brought him to the ground quite harshly, breaking his arm in the meantime. The woman was in no fit state to run. She just slumped to the floor unconscious, but getting this rapist off the streets was the priority. I managed to cuff him before checking on the female and called for an ambulance."

"What about backup?" Martha interjected again.

"One of my many regrets. I wanted to solve the case and save the day without help. I feared others taking the credit for finding and arresting him, meaning I would miss out on a possible promotion. So I didn't call it in. I wanted to march him down to the police station myself and take all the glory."

"So what went wrong?"

"Everything. Everything went wrong. I let him talk. I watched him cry. A truly broken man."

"Are we still talking about the serial rapist?"

"I know. I thought I could maybe rehabilitate him. Get another scumbag off the streets by not putting him behind a cell to rot and become a pointless waste of life."

"He was a serial rapist! He was already a pointless waste of life!" Nick growled.

"Yes, I know. But I was young and full of it. I thought I could fix anyone and anything. And so I tried. I got him his new identity on the condition that he would break no more laws, and that women would no longer be his prey. He had 6 victims ready to come forward and oust him, but they all backed out simultaneously. I had no idea why, but that was the break we needed. With no victims or witnesses, Scot Guilds became Scotty Branning. A new identity, a new beginning. His past was not reported and so he ceased to exist and Scotty was born, reportedly living off the grid until most recent times.

"I put my job at risk for him, and it was the worst decision I had ever made. After what I thought was a success, he eventually went back to his roots and started attacking women again. I managed to track him down on the side, once again leaving out any kind of backup. A stupid, amateur move. Through the confrontation he attacked me. But he wasn't alone. Jason Stark made his appearance. Scotty had joined a gang, and together they almost beat the life out of me. I thought it would never end, and I was certain I was going to die. Thankfully they left me alive, on one condition. I would leave Scotty alone, and never breathe a word of his crimes or those of the gang. I also learnt that Jason paid a visit to the 6 victims of Scotty and threatened them at gunpoint if they were to testify his guilt. Through fear, they pulled out, and that was the start of the gang. Then came the ultimatum. I would keep my mouth shut, otherwise, my family, my wife and daughter, would be tortured in front of me, and then murdered. And then, it would be my turn. I couldn't risk my family's safety. I agreed to their terms, rushed myself to hospital. Said I got into a fight with some stranger. They fixed me up, and that night I booked one-way tickets to America and ran away with my family. Of course, they know none of this. They questioned the move but eventually just accepted that I had had enough of work and fancied a change. They bought it in the end, and one day they just simply stopped asking, and I never heard from Scotty, Jason, or the gang since. Well, until last week when I was catching up on the news in the UK which I do every couple of months. Just to see home again. That's when I saw the picture of Scotty and the report of his death, and his involvement in the rape and murder of Lisa. I felt sick. I couldn't believe what he had done. And to then be murdered himself? I argued with myself whether to call you or not because, in a way, this whole thing could have been avoided if I just called for backup the first time I had met Scotty. I could have prevented Lisa's death. And now I have to live with that every day, for the rest of my life."

"And so you should!" Nick barked, anger cursing through his veins.

"So you thought you could go behind the law and rehabilitate a serial rapist, but all it really achieved was more rapes and now murder, too?" Martha asked in confirmation.

"I know what I did was wrong and I truly wish I could change it, but I can't. But if this information can help with your case in any way then it would have been worth it. Just please keep my name out of this. My family could be in big danger if you breathe a word of my involvement, so please, as much as you hate and resent me right now, please just keep to your word and keep me out of this. Good luck!" And within that second, before Martha or Nick could reply, the phone went completely dead. The detectives stared at each other silently. No words could even begin to explain what had just happened.

* * *

The two detectives were still in the interrogation room, trying to make heads or tails of the current situation. Kevin was still being held in interrogation room 1, along with his extremely inpatient lawyer who was starting to demand that someone either interview his client or let him go. The commotion was easily heard through the walls of the station; thin and cold compared to the MSMI Bureau not too far up the road, but at least the interrogation rooms themselves were quite warm. *Probably due to the dark painted walls keeping the heat in,* Martha thought.

"Let's go and put that lawyer out of his misery and see how he can get Kevin out of this one," Martha suggested.

CHAPTER TWENTY

Martha, Nick, Kevin, and his lawyer, Pete Stuart, were all gathered within interrogation room 1.

"Look, I don't know how many times I have to tell you, I did *not* kill Lisa! I loved her!"

"Oh, we know you loved her. A little more than a normal person loves, though."

"And what is that supposed to mean?" Pete interrupted.

"For the record of the tape, the MSMI Department was granted a warrant to take and search Kevin's computer." Martha began. "On this computer, we found a one-way ticket booked for Australia, the same place our victim was running away to. In addition to this, we also found a poem that seems to contain a death threat, once again, towards our victim, Lisa Marsh."

"It was just a poem, man! I didn't mean any harm."

"Why did you book yourself a one-way ticket to Australia?" Nick asked, frowning.

"Because she was leaving and I couldn't live without her! I had to follow her. We were meant to be together!"

"How did you know she was running away."

"No comment."

"Why? Do you have something to hide?" He pushed.

"No comment."

"We have your laptop, Kevin. There is nothing you can hide from us. Our computer analysis team will find anything you're keeping from us, and that will only reflect badly on you if you don't come forward now!" Martha explained.

"No comment."

Before either Nick or Martha could ask another question, there was a knock on the door. Upon opening, Michael Lance walked in.

"Detectives, I need you to take a look at something." He walked back out of the room. Martha suspended the interview and paused the tape, and then with her partner, she followed Michael out of the interrogation room and into Michaels temporary office based within the police station.

Michaels office was a great deal smaller than his one in the MSMI building. The police station felt rather lacking compared to the new build bureau that the team had been so used to over the few years. Apparently, new interrogation rooms were in planning for the bureau which would help the MSMI team to undergo their investigations in much more suitable environments, leaving the police station for the police officers and petty crime.

"What you got?" Nick asked.

"I've figured out how he found out about her plan to run away."

"Go on . . ." Martha pushed.

"It seems our stalker dabbles in computer hacking in his spare time."

"Meaning?"

"Kevin has managed to hack Lisa's computer and for a good couple of months, he has been able to see absolutely everything on her computer, even down to watching it live. He also had access to her webcam where he has collected more unsolicited pictures of our victim."

"The son of a fucking bitch!" Nick growled.

I'm starting to believe that's his favourite saying, Martha thought to herself, trying to stifle a very badly timed giggle.

"Needless to say that's how he found out about Lisa running away to Australia. He purchased his ticket approximately 1 hour after Lisa bought hers."

"Anything else?"

"His search history. One week before Lisa's abduction, he googled "how to commit the perfect murder", "how to make someone fall in love with you", and "how to hide a body". Now to me, this speaks volumes about his plan once he got his hands on her."

"Right, I'm not taking 'No Comment' as a fucking answer anymore. Lawyer or not, I will beat the truth out of that little shit face, if it's the last thing I do." By this point, Nick's anger was so powerful that Martha and Michael could sense the vibe through their very souls. Kevin will truly wish he was never born.

* * *

"Interview resumed at 19:07, currently present are myself, Detective Martha Willis, my partner, Detective Nick Hardy, and Kevin Linn with his lawyer Mr Pete Stewart. Now, Kevin, we have some very intriguing information that has come from your computer. Do you have any idea what it is that we could have found? I would urge you to speak the truth."

"I haven't any idea what you're on about." He grumbled.

"Hey Google, how do you commit the perfect murder? How do you hide a body? Does any of this ring a bell to you?"

"It's not what it looks like!" He gasped, as though he was struggling for air.

"Oh really?" Nick asked angrily.

"I suggest you do not answer these questions, Kevin," Pete interjected, but his client wasn't listening.

"I swear, I just searched it because I was interested. I would never hurt my Lisa. My precious Lisa."

"So you searched it because you wanted to know out of interest, not out of the intent of murdering someone? That's a pretty hard pill to swallow." Martha continued.

"I swear it's the truth!"

"Tell me this then, why did you hack into her computer? Why were you watching her every move."

"You can't prove that!"

"Ah, but we can. You see, you left everything on your computer logged in so everything was easily found by our analysis team. We have screenshots that you took of Lisa without her consent, through her webcam while she was undressing. More private photography added to what was already on the wall in your apartment. This is a severe case of stalking and you are going to end up behind bars after this interrogation whether you confess or not. Now, this is your final chance to tell us what you were doing spying on Lisa Marsh."

"I loved her. I wanted to protect her. She was in danger from Jason. He would hurt her all the time. I have evidence."

"Such as?" Nick pursued.

"I have footage from her webcam saved onto my computer, but it's encrypted."

"Our team will find that soon enough. Why is it so important?"

"He raped her! It was all on camera. They were having a fight, he knocked her unconscious and then raped her! I felt so useless."

"So you just sat back and let it happen?"

"He has a gang! There was nothing I could do. Her mum had no idea what was happening under her own roof. And if I told her she'd soon forget anyway."

"When was this?" Martha asked.

"About a week before she went missing."

"So around the same time, you googled how to get away with murder?

114

The same time you wrote a death threat in a poem?"

"It's not like that!"

"Then please, enlighten us. Because from where we are sitting, you're looking more and more suspicious."

"I offered Lisa to kill Jason, to set her free. She thought I was mad at first but then eventually came round to the idea. I started Googling how to kill someone and get rid of the body so I could get rid of Jason once and for all."

"And why didn't you go ahead with the murder?"

"Lisa started to chicken out. She said she still loved him and didn't want him dead. I got angry and that's when I wrote the poem. I wanted to tell her how much she meant to me, and that if Jason is left to live then she would be the one to die. With the way he was beating her she wouldn't have had long left. But the poem changed nothing. She booked a ticket to run away to Australia and stupidly told Jason about it. He wouldn't let her go free, he would follow her and kill her. So I booked a ticket to go, too, so I could be there to stop him from killing her upon arrival. You may think I'm a sick stalker but I had all her best interests at heart, and her safety was my priority."

"And the unsolicited nudes that she didn't consent to?"

"That I am guilty of. She was so beautiful, her body a work of pure art. She was made to perfection, and I loved her."

"Well whether you meant well or not, I'm afraid we are going to have to arrest you."

"What? On what charges?" He yelped.

"Stalking, illegally taken images, murder intent. You're going to be behind bars for, at the very least, a few months." Nick growled lowly.

"Can they do that?" He begged his lawyer.

"Yes, they can. And that's why you should have stuck to no comment." He sighed, clearly agitated with his client.

CHAPTER TWENTY-ONE

"**D**o you buy his story?**"** Nick asked.

"I'm not sure. He seemed genuine, but with all those pictures, the poem, the stalking, it's difficult to believe he meant no harm toward her. Especially after seeing him punch her on CCTV." Martha sighed. "There is one thing I'm sure about, though."

"What's that?"

"Jason is definitely involved in the kidnapping of Lisa. Maybe not the murder, and maybe he didn't kidnap her himself, but I am certain he is involved somehow. Michael Lance has confirmed that an encrypted video of Jason raping Lisa was found on Kevin's computer. If he is capable of doing that to her after knocking her unconscious, he is more than capable of kidnapping her, alibi or not!"

"We'll bring him in if we can find something that can prove his involvement. We will also interrogate him in regards to him raping Lisa; show him the recording that proves him guilty. And while we're on the topic, let's track down the 6 rape victims of Scotty's and see if they will testify against Jason for obstructing the course justice through threatening behaviour. And I wouldn't be surprised if he played a part in Scotty's murder, either, especially knowing he was the one who purchased the deadly dose of Liquid Meth." Nick concluded.

Martha's phone began to ring. Muhammad Muskhan. "Hello? Yup, brilliant. We're on our way!" She put the phone down. "That was the boss. The 4 members of Jason's gang are currently taking up 4 interrogation rooms downstairs. Ready?"

"Oh yes!" He smirked, and they both left their office, locking the door behind them.

* * *

"Shawn Rose," Nick began.

"Yup." He grunted.

"Was you a member of Jason's gang?"

"I guess so."

"A simple yes or no would suffice."

"Fine, yes."

"Do you know Scotty Branning?"

"Obviously! He was a member, too."

"And a Zahid Maul?"

"A bit, yeah. He'd deal us some gear. Is this because of the drugs?"

"Are you aware that Jason's girlfriend was kidnapped, raped and then murdered? Only for Scotty to then die due to a forced overdose through drugs purchased by your little gang from Zahid?"

"I have seen a bit on the news but weren't really payin' that much attention."

"You weren't paying attention to what your own mates were up to?"

"Nope, and I have nothin' to do with the drugs that killed Scotty either!" He said firmly. "Jason was always the one who dealt with that side of things, the rest of us just followed."

"So Jason bought the liquid meth that killed Scotty?" Martha asked.

"I dunno, I guess. I genuinely have no idea."

"Is there anything you do know?" Nick was growing agitated.

"Not really. And I don't want to say anythin' that will get me in shit with Jason or the law! So if you want to carry on questioning me then I want a lawyer."

"No, it's fine. You can go." Martha said. "But we'll be keeping a close eye on things." Martha suspended the interview and left the room with Nick, onto the next one.

"Clyde Bennet, are you a member of Jason's gang?" Nick asked.

"Yes."

"Were you, or any of the members of this gang, involved in the kidnapping, rape and murder of Lisa Marsh, and the murder of Scotty Branning?"

"Not that I'm aware of." He said bluntly, rolling his eyes in annoyance.

"Did you handle any drugs relating to Zahid Maul, such as liquid meth?"

"Drugs were Jason's department. Everyone knows that."

"Where were you the night of Lisa's murder?"

"In bed."

"And when she was kidnapped?"

"Pub, probably."

"Did you rape Lisa Marsh?" Martha stepped in.

"Am I going to need a lawyer?"

"Why, feeling guilty are we?"

"I know my rights, and I know you have nothing on me, so let me go, or give me a lawyer!" He snapped. Unfortunately for the detectives, Clyde was right. They really didn't have anything on him or the rest of the gang members. They suspended the interview and let him walk free. 2 down, 2 to go.

"Royce Arnold, was you involved in the kidnapping of Lisa Marsh?"

Martha asked.

"Hell no I wasn't, but I knew about it!" He replied rapidly.

Did he seriously just admit to knowing about her kidnapping? "What exactly do you know?"

"Jason needed money, and this was his quick fix. Not entirely his idea, mind you."

"Who's idea was it?"

"I dunno who she was, but he certainly liked her, at least for a little while anyway. He gets bored easily."

Is he really singing like a fucking canary? "Was you or anyone you know of involved in the rape of Lisa Marsh?"

"Honestly? We all had a bit! She was easy! Barely let out a peep. Although she was occasionally gagged if she didn't do as she was told."

"Who gagged her?"

"Jason. He needed to keep her under control so no one would hear her and find her. He was making a mint, I tell ya!"

"Why are you telling us all this?" Nick asked, just as confused as Martha.

"Because the fucking bastard tried it on with my sister! She's fucking 9! If there is anything I can do to get him behind bars, then I will fucking do it. Even if it means dropping myself in it. We all had a bit of Lisa, as well as complete strangers I'd never seen before. I don't know why he needed money, but if you find that woman he was with, she would know exactly what went down."

"You do realise we are going to have to keep you in, at least overnight? And we need a written confession if you're willing to confess to raping Lisa."

"I know, I know. Get us the paperwork and let's get done with it."

"Interview suspended at 19:20. Thank you." Martha said, and then left the room with Nick.

"I genuinely can't believe what just happened there!" Martha said open-mouthed, in a state of shock.

"Tell me about it! That was fucking easy! Why can't all criminals hand themselves in like that? Would make our lives a lot easier."

"I know we still don't have much on Jason, especially with that alibi of his, but we are definitely starting to build a case that could bring him down."

"Indeed. Onto the next one?"

"Keegan Lloyd, are you a member of Jason's gang?" Nick asked.

"Who? No." He answered short but quick.

"But we have eye-witnesses that say otherwise."

"They lie. Keep me outta this shit!"

"This is a murder investigation and you are part of the gang involved, there is no keeping you out of it!" Nick barked.

"Well, tough fucking shit 'cause I know nothin'!" He crossed his arms in a huff.

Yeah, we're getting nothing from this one.

"Don't think you're going anywhere anytime soon, mate. You're going to be here a while!" Nick suspended the interview and guided Martha to the exit.

"I reckon he is going to be the toughest one to crack," Nick said, analysing Keegan through the window of the door to the interrogation room.

"Agreed. Call it a night?"

"Yeah. It's been a long day. Home it is!"

* * *

It was 23:00 by the time Martha finally got home. The night was dark and cold, and thankfully the heating was left on throughout the day so Martha could unwind with a hot chocolate by the fire before bed. It had been decided by the MSMI Bureau to collect more evidence against Jason before making an official arrest. While staring into the fire, Martha couldn't help but think about the victims of Scotty, what they must have gone through to come forward about the rapes, to then be threatened at gunpoint to keep their mouths shut. She couldn't even begin to imagine what effect that must have had on the rest of their lives to date. It was Michael Lance's job to hopefully track the victims down in order to prepare a possible interview with each one of them so they could get Jason behind bars for as long as humanly possible, and hopefully the gang members, too.

How could anyone do such a horrid thing, and then go on to threaten them for their silence? Her thoughts were running at 100 miles per hour, she couldn't stop the racing.

The night was drawing in, and before she knew it, it was 3:00 am. *Bloody hell.* She lay in her bed. She had been tossing and turning for the past two hours, praying for sleep, anger growing towards herself. *Just go to fucking sleep!*

Creak!

What the fuck was that? She shot up instantly. A floorboard outside of her bedroom had creaked. *It's just the apartment settling,* she tried to convince herself, but she failed. She grabbed for her phone on the bedside cabinet and her handgun that lay next to it. She dialled Nick's number, balanced the phone between her chin and shoulder, and then readied her gun, aiming at her bedroom door. *I'm not willing to take any chances.*

"Hey, Martha. It's 3 in the morning, what's up?" He was audibly groggy.

"I heard movement in my hallway. I don't know if someone is in my apartment or if I'm just being paranoid." She whispered gently, voice shaking.

"Hey, it's okay. I'll be there in ten. You got your gun handy?"

"Yes, ready and waiting to fire if needs be."

"Right, I'll be as quick as I can." The phone went dead.

The minutes felt long and drawn out, her arm aching from holding the gun up while so tense. *Come on, Nick. I need you.* She prayed.

The front door clicked. Footsteps started, first in the living room, then the hallway, then the toilet, the spare room, and then they started towards Martha's bedroom. *Oh god, oh god.* Her hand grew shakier. The door handle slowly pulled down. The hinges creaked.

"STAY BACK OR I'LL SHOOT!" She screamed.

Nick's head darted around the door, "NO! It's me! It's only me!" He called.

"Oh my god, Nick!" She jumped out of her bed and into his arms, embracing him like the saviour she felt he was. "I was going to shoot you!"

"Well let's be glad you didn't! I've checked the entire apartment, no one is here but us two."

"Are you sure?"

"Yes."

"How sure?"

"100%. I promise!"

She hugged him again in relief. "Would you like a hot drink?"

"No thanks. I just need to know that you're okay?"

"I am now. Could I ask a favour?"

"Sure."

"Would you mind staying over? Just a few nights, so I can get settled again, rather than spending every waking minute alone and scared?"

"What happened to being okay on your own?" He giggled softly. "Of course I'll stay. You don't even have to ask."

"Thank you! Honestly, it means a lot." She sighed gratefully. *What would I do without you? You're seriously perfect. Right, come on, snap out of it girl, you nearly blew his head off 5 seconds ago.* "I'll just set up the bed in the spare room."

"I'll give you a hand."

CHAPTER TWENTY-TWO

The case of Lisa's murder had hit day 34. Martha and Nick sat in their office in the MSMI Bureau. Their computers were on and the whiteboard was covered in pictures of silhouettes, ready for the 6 rape victims of Scotty to be identified.

"If we find out who these women are, we can bring them the justice they deserve, along with Lisa. We need to identify who the second rapist is, then we would most likely be looking at her murderer, too, or at least someone who played a part, along with Jason himself." Martha said aloud whilst typing on her computer. Both detectives found themselves searching through old case files and exchanging private emails with Officer Karl Wright to confirm the identities and whereabouts of the 6 rape victims.

The office phone began to ring. Karl Wright was on the other end.

"I've got the list of the victims." He confirmed to the detectives whilst on speakerphone.

"Great, alphabetical order, please," Nick replied.

"The first victim is Adele Gonzalez. She was 17 when she was raped, so that makes her roughly 24 years old now. The second victim is Anya Vaughn, 22 then, approximately 29 now. The third victim was Beth Bray. 30 then, 37 now. The fourth victim was known as Charlotte Clintell. 19 years old, now 26. Fifth and sixth victims were Nadia Pugh, 20, and Spencer Church, also 20, making them both around 27."

"Any information on their current situation?" Martha asked while Nick wrote their names under the pictured silhouettes posted on the whiteboard.

"Unfortunately that's all the information I have on my end. Hopefully, the NCLB UK Database will be of more use to you than me."

"You've helped massively, we now have a starting point. Thank you!"

"No problem. Talk to you later. Keep me posted."

"Will do." Martha hung up the phone.

"How could you be so calm with him when it's all his fault?" Nick asked in disbelief.

"It's difficult but necessary and professional."

"You have the patience of a saint." He smiled and then winked at her.

Heart, feel free to slow down. She thought, trying to calm the butterflies Nick had just given her. She began running the names through the NCLB UK – National Criminal Law Bureau – database. Although the database was part of the Criminal Law, anyone who was involved in a crime, either committing it, reporting it, or simply a victim to it, they would appear in this database thereafter. This enabled cases like this to find victims or criminals who had gone off-grid after a crime was committed, or even those who stayed on the grid, to make research on cases easier and quicker, with everything compiled into one place.

* * *

Adele Gonzalez reported rape crime against her at the age of 17. Withdrew complaint a week later. Committed suicide at the age of 19. Reported to have struggled with her mental health after making rape allegations against Scot Guilds.

Anya Vaughn reported one Scot Guilds had raped her at the age of 22. Her report was later withdrawn. She is currently 29 and has had trouble with the law since becoming a prostitute. She has been arrested twice for allegedly assaulting two of her clients. Neither case went ahead, for the victims withdrew their complaints.

Beth Bray, aged 30 when reporting a rape allegation against Scot Guilds. Her rape allegation was pulled a week after being made. She is now 37 years old and is serving a 5-year prison sentence for possession of drugs with the intent of dealing.

Charlotte Clintel, aged 19 when reporting a case of rape by Scot Guilds. It was reported that she was once threatened at gunpoint to withdraw her rape allegations against Scot Guilds, but after sobering up she withdrew these new claims, and there was no evidence to prove otherwise. At the age of 24, 5 years after the allegations were made, Charlotte Clintel was found hanging in her bedsit. She was pronounced dead at the scene. The coroner confirmed suicide.

Nadia Pugh was 20 years old when she claimed she was raped by Scot Guilds. After one week, she withdrew the report, claiming she had been mistaken and that the rape was actually consensual intercourse. She is now 27 years old and works as a councillor for rape victims. Unfortunately, she has repeated run-ins with the law for anti-social behaviour due to an ongoing addiction to alcohol.

Spencer Church, aged 20 when allegedly raped, complaint withdrawn after approximately one week. To date, she has battled with an addiction to cocaine and has been homeless since she was 21. She is now 27 and is reportedly in and out of homeless shelters, and is trying to get herself clean with the help of Narcotics Anonymous.

* * *

"This is some heart-wrenching stuff," Martha concluded after reading the reports aloud to Nick.

"Tell me about it. 1 lost to suicide, 3 addicts, 1 homeless, and 1 a prostitute."

"I just can't believe how much Scotty and Jason have completely ruined their entire lives. I wonder how they would have turned out if they were never threatened to keep quiet, or better yet, never raped!"

"They were so brave to come forward, and all it did was make it worse for them. What does that say about our justice system?"

"The officers should have put them under victim support and trans-ferred them to a safe-house in order to let the case go to trial. I know they couldn't do much due to them withdrawing their reports, but surely something could have been done sooner to get Scotty and Jason off the streets."

"Well, we're here now, and we are going to make sure that this will never happen again. They don't deserve their freedom."

"It would be extremely advantageous if the remaining women would be willing to testify against them now. They will probably decline because they are all at a point in life where it is all becoming too much for them, causing self-destruction, but it's worth a try. Lisa needs justice, too." Martha said sternly.

CHAPTER TWENTY-THREE

"**M**artha, Nick," Tazmin called into the room.

Great, Taz is here. What does she want now? "Yeah?"

"There's someone in the lobby waiting to speak to you both. Her name is Leanne Baker."

"Leanne's here?" Nick asked, confused.

"Bring her through."

As Tazmin disappeared behind the office door, a timid looking Leanne walked in and took a seat opposite the two detectives.

"Hi, Miss Baker, how can we help?"

"I saw on the news, about a Scotty Branning?" She began.

"Yes, what about him?" Nick's eyebrows were raised with concern.

"I knew him. We'd been friends for a few years."

"Oh, I'm so sorry you had to find out that way." Martha consoled.

"No, it's okay. We weren't exactly the closest of friends."

"Why not?" Nick pursued.

"He was into drugs and stuff and partying. Not really my kind of thing." She sniffled and blew her nose into a tissue she had pulled from her coat pocket. Her eyes were watering like she was ready to cry.

"At the risk of sounding rude, what is the purpose of your visit?"

"A few hours before I found Lisa's body, he phoned me. He said he was over the moon, that he'd got his end away with this chick and she just lay there and let him. He said it was a threesome like he had ever had before. He always bragged about this stuff when he was high, and I was always on the receiving end of the phone. I think he did it to try and make me jealous. Anyway, he mentioned the other man's name. It was someone called John McKennith. I didn't think anything of it until the news report said about Scotty raping the same woman I had found dead, and that someone else had done so too, but his DNA wasn't on file and there were no witnesses. It got me thinking, maybe this John guy that Scotty was talking about on the phone was the other rapist, and what if it was Lisa's rape that Scotty was telling me about?" She started to cry. "I mean, I literally heard my own friend brag about raping someone shortly before she died. Does that make him the murderer? If he and his mate were the last ones to see her alive, and they did that to her? And on top of that, they left her naked in the streets for me to find, and I will never get that image out of my head!" She pulled more tissue from her coat pocket and began dabbing it around her eyes, trying to fight her running mascara that was slowly leaving black streaks down her cheeks.

"Why didn't you tell us all of this before?" Nick pressed on.

"Because none of it made sense or clicked until I saw that news report. I feel sick!"

"Hey, it's okay." Martha got up and moved to the end of the table where Leanne was seated. "It's okay. You've done brilliantly, coming all the way here to tell us this. You're strong, and you have been a great help with this case. The information you have given us today is vital. We can't thank you enough." She hugged Leanne. A Few minutes after she had calmed down, Martha signalled Tazmin to come back in and help Leanne find her way back out of the MSMI Bureau.

"John McKennith. That's the first time his name has come up in this case. What do you reckon?" Martha asked, intrigued.

"I reckon we should get a warrant to take his DNA and test it against the DNA found on Lisa's body. I'm betting it will be a match."

"Hopefully Michael can find us his address."

"Ah, my two favourite detectives. Leanne spoke to me before you guys, so I'm all over it!" Michael announced whilst walking into their office.

"Speak of the devil. Any luck?" Martha stood, shortly followed by Nick.

"Indeed. He lives a 15-minute drive away from the scene of the crime. And that's not the only news I've got for you."

"Well go on then, keeping us in suspense." Nick pushed.

"Jessica told me to inform you that we have the location that Lisa was held hostage in."

"Seriously?" Martha almost squealed, over the moon with the news that the case was finally moving forward.

"Yup, seriously. And it's looking like an abandoned warehouse in London, once known as 'Lloyds Machinery Packing Co, in E3. I've emailed both addresses to you."

"How do we know it's the same place Lisa was held hostage?" Nick asked, eyes wide.

"Jessica said the particulates that she found within Lisa's lungs consisted of soot, dust, and dirt, along with some fly ash and carbon which has been found in this particular location, due to a small fire that was reported the night before Lisa was murdered."

"They started a fire?"

"Indeed. Our team has given it a once over and said it looked to be a bonfire that they were participating in. Now it's just an empty warehouse. Whoever was using it is long gone now."

"Well, looks like we'll be visiting the warehouse as well as the mysterious John McKennith. Thank you, Michael." Martha said with a smile of relief.

"No problem. Now go catch us some scum and get them off the street once and for all."

130

"We will do," Martha and Nick replied simultaneously.

* * *

It was 13:00 by the time Martha Willis and Nick Hardy arrived at the warehouse in which Lisa was being held hostage. The bitterly cold weather was still felt indoors, biting at their faces and leaving the tips of their noses red. It was as though the agents were still out in the open. The concrete walls were mostly stained ash black, insinuating a large fire took place. The floor was covered in puddles due to the leaking black ceiling, and the pillars and roof beams looked as though they could have given way at any point, despite being given the all-clear on Health and Safety checks before the detective's arrivals. Forensics was due in about an hour. In the meantime, the warehouse belonged to the detectives.

A lone plastic school-like chair sat in the middle of the warehouse, the centrepiece that Lisa found herself tied to for two weeks. The rotting rope that kept her in place was still wrapped around the chair, looking like a crime scene you'd see on a TV Show. The smell of smoke and weed pricked at Martha's nose and forced its way into her airways.

"That stench!" She moaned, "It feels so fresh like this whole kidnap happened mare hours ago."

"I know what you mean. It's completely deserted, but I can still feel Lisa's presence."

"I can't even begin to imagine the fear she must have been feeling."

Not far from the chair was a metal bin that was used for the bonfire that took place. The building was practically empty, yet it still had life, its own story, and unfortunately, it ended with Lisa Marsh.

"So, what do we reckon happened on her last day. How did she end up leaving this place and end up in an alleyway not far from here, completely naked and lifeless?" Nicked posed for Martha.

Slowly, Martha headed toward the chair in the middle of the warehouse and sat down. "Let's find out." She wrapped her arms around the back of the chair, starting a self-roleplay in her mind. She closed her eyes.

"*I am Lisa. I am tied to the chair. I cannot move. I have no clothes on. Why? Maybe I'm being used for sex, which would explain why there is more than one lot of DNA on my body. I am a living sex slave. Men come and go, and I can't do a thing to stop them. My clothes have been partially burnt in a bonfire they held. I prayed the smoke would bring in investigators, but it went unnoticed. Why? Because I am in a deserted, secluded area in London, no one around to save me. It's been a very long time. I don't know how long. I've been held here long enough for it to feel like an eternity. I need to get out. A customer comes to have their fill, but he makes the mistake of untying me. I kick him in the balls, dart for the exit. I don't care that I'm naked or that there is snow on the ground. All I care about is my freedom. I can feel the fresh air on my face, in my lungs. Freedom.*

"*OUCH! I'm being pulled to the ground. He has caught me, him and his friend. I hit my head hard on the pavement, and I am raped once again.*"

Martha opened her tear-filled eyes, wiping one drop away. She came to stand, and Nick embraced her. "It's okay," he said in her ear, gently.

She pulled away from the hug. "There were three of them."

"Pardon?"

"Two customers, one being Scotty, the other probably being our mysterious John McKennith. They raped her while she was alive. I don't know if she was awake or unconscious, but that's when it happened, in the alley. They left her alive. She was killed by a third person at the scene."

"What do you mean? What makes you think that? We have no evidence to prove it." Nick was visibly confused.

"I saw some fabric hanging out of the metal bin when we walked in.

I'm presuming it's Lisa's clothes, an attempt to get rid of the evidence. That would explain why she was found naked with no clothes at the scene of the crime. And there's an earring on the floor by the chair, and it looks as though it has blood on it."

"And?"

"Lisa didn't have any piercings. There was a woman here. We need to get that earring to Jessica and find out who this mystery woman is!"

CHAPTER TWENTY-FOUR

Martha and Nick stood by Jessica Heath as she examined **the earring** through a microscope. "Well, it's definitely blood, but whose? I am going to have to take a swab and compare it to our victim and the NCLB Database. It will take a while before I can get back to you about a match."

"Thank you, Jessica. Give us a call when you get anything back." Martha said. The two detectives left the Forensics Lab and headed for the building's exit, to Nicks car.

"How did you work out that she was being used as a sex slave?"

"I remembered Jessica saying at the beginning of the case that Lisa suffered multiple cases of sexual abuse. With at least two people confirmed for the night of her death, that means more took place in the lead up to her demise. To me, that indicates a serious case of sex slavery. I put myself into her mind and it all just clicks into place. A dark place, but a place none-the-less." Martha looked visibly sad, and Nick knew exactly why. Her past couldn't have made this case any easier.

"Can't believe you found the bloody earring before Forensics got a chance to look. You have got the perfect eyes."

A smile grew upon Martha's lips instantly, and she could feel her cheeks burning red with embarrassment and shyness. *How does he do it, every time, he just manages to make everything better.*

The detectives arrived at Jason's flat. By this point they had lost count of how many times they had visited him; only this time, he would be going back to the station in their custody. Jason opened the front door, his face burning red with anger, his eyes rolling, mouth ready to kick off some screams and swears, but he didn't get the chance. Within seconds, Nick had spun Jason around and cuffed his arms behind his back.

"Jason Stark, I'm arresting you on the suspicion of kidnap and imprisonment. You do not have to say anything, but it may harm your defence if you do not mention when questioned something which you may later rely on in court. Anything you do say may be given in evidence."

"Kidnap? Fucking kidnap!?" And with that, Nick forced Jason to walk towards their vehicle and pushed his head down and threw him into the back seat.

* * *

"Why didn't you report your girlfriend missing?" Martha questioned him.

"I didn't fucking realise she was missing. I didn't exactly watch her every move."

"Maybe not. I assume you're going to tell us you loved her and respected her?"

"Obviously. She was my girl!"

"So why did you rape her?"

"Rape? I never fucking raped her!" He stood up in anger, fists smashing hard against the cold metal table that separated him from the detectives. Nick lunged forwards and forced Jason back into his seat.

"For the purpose of the tape, I am now showing Mr Stark video footage from evidence 12-0-B."

As the footage played, Jason looked on and watched as he knocked Lisa out with a punch to the face, throwing her onto her bed, and then proceeding to rape her whilst unconscious and unable to consent.

"Where the fuck did you get that?"

"Can you confirm that is you in the video?"

"Yes, but – "

"And that is you forcing sexual moves onto an unconscious Lisa, unable to consent?"

"It wasn't like that! She would have said yes if she was awake!"

"But she wasn't though, was she?" Martha yelled. "She was unconscious and you took advantage of her, and that, Mr Stark, is illegal!"

"Fine, I raped her! But I never fucking killed her!"

"You might not have killed her, you might not have raped her time and time again in the warehouse, but that doesn't mean to say you didn't kidnap her!"

"I didn't. I didn't kidnap her!"

"So where were you the day she was kidnapped?"

"Why don't you leave me the fuck alone and ask someone who fucking cares? I did nothing to her, end of!"

"You see, Jason, we don't believe you!" Nick interrupted.

"That's your problem, mate!"

"The only problem here is that you're a rapist scumbag who never reported his own girlfriend missing for two weeks. Two fucking weeks! It took until her mother with Alzheimer's reported it, and half the time she doesn't even remember her daughter, let alone remember her disappearance and murder. You don't even have a shred of decency in you, to tell the truth. This poor woman was kidnapped, raped, and murdered, and all you care about is saving your own fucking arse!"

"I. Didn't. Kidnap. Lisa. Got it?" He mocked, almost casual, and ever so slightly cocky.

"Who's John McKennith?" Martha asked.

"What's it to you?"

"Well, if you must know, a witness has come forward to report him as Lisa's second rapist shortly before she died."

"That fucking cunt!"

"Know him, then?"

"He's supposed to be my best mate if you must know! He said he'd not touch her! I was going to find him some other chick!"

"You what?" Nick called.

"Nothing! I didn't mean anything!"

"Sounds as though you know something you're not telling us."

"I want a lawyer."

"I bet you do!"

"And a deal . . ."

CHAPTER TWENTY-FIVE

"**W**hat should we do?" **Martha asked Nick,** both of them back in their office at the MSMI Bureau.

"I guess we wait and see what Mohammad says."

Mohammad Muskhan, father to Tazmin Muskhan – Taz –, was in charge of the MSMI Agency, and it was his job to look over any cases and interfere when plea deals would come through.

"Well, while we wait, I'm just going to give Tyler a call." She pulled her phone to her ear and waited for a few rings. After the 10th ring, the phone went straight to voicemail. "Hey, Tyler, it's Martha. Just letting you know I'm staying at my place now. Nick is staying for a bit until I feel safe and settled again. Give me a call when you get this. Lots of love." She hung up the phone and sighed, placing it into her pocket.

"What's up?"

"I don't know. It's just she never misses a call. She's always glued to her phone."

"She must be pretty busy then."

"Maybe."

"Just remember she is pregnant, she might be at the midwives or something."

"True." The door to their office knocked, followed shortly by Mohammad, walking into the room slowly.

"So, what's the deal?" He asked.

"Jason will plead guilty to rape and tell us what really happened to Lisa, in favour of a lesser sentence in an open prison."

"Fuck me." He replied, sighing heavily.

"Tell me about it," Nick said.

"No admittance to murder?"

"Nope. He has an airtight alibi, and he's sticking to it."

"Reckon he knows who the murderer is?"

"Possibly. And he might know what happened to Scotty, too."

"But he isn't offering that information? Just a guilty plea to kidnap."

"Yup."

"Okay. See if he will agree to tell *everything* he knows about her murder and what happened to Scotty. Try and get the whereabouts of Mr McKennith, and what they were doing in the warehouse for the two weeks Lisa was missing. We may have a rough idea, but nothing beats a confirmation from the perpetrator himself. It won't stand in court otherwise. Don't force him to, because an admission under threat also won't stand up in court. If you can get this information from him willingly, we will look into allowing him a sentence in an open prison."

"Are we sure we want him in an open prison?" Martha asked.

"If we can uncover the entire case through it, then yes. Head back to the station now and see what you can do."

"Yes, sir." Martha and Nick said simultaneously.

* * *

"Jason Stark," Martha began. "We have a proposition for you, and it's entirely your choice."

"Okay?" He said, raising an eyebrow.

"We want to know everything you know. When and how Lisa was

kidnapped, why she was kidnapped, what happened over the course of the two weeks that she was held hostage in, the lead up to her death, and how she died. We want a confession, information on anyone and everyone involved, including your gang's involvement, and then we will see about letting you serve your sentence in an open prison." Martha explained.

"But I don't know how she died."

"Are you willing to take a lie detector test? It won't be used in court, but it will give us an idea of what you're telling us is true or not."

"Fine, yes! I'll do the fucking lie detector test."

* * *

Michael Lance, head of computing and analysis, set up the lie detector test within the hour before finally letting Jason and the two detectives into his office. The room was bleak and bare. No photos on the walls, an off white carpet, and steamed-up windows that looked to be blown. It took a few minutes to attach all of the wires to Jason before the test could begin. A monitor was placed on his chest, strapped around his body with thin wires, a blood pressure band was wrapped around his arm, and finally, an Oximeter Blood Oxygen Saturation Monitor with Pulse Rate readings was clipped to his index finger.

"We're all set," Michael confirmed.

"Ready?" Martha asked Jason.

"I guess."

"Is your name Jason Stark?"

"Yes."

"Are you 29 years old?"

"Yes."

CHAPTER TWENTY-FIVE

"Was you involved in the kidnapping of Lisa Marsh?"

"Yes."

"Do you have a pet dog?"

"No."

"Did you deal drugs to Scotty Branning?"

"No."

"Did you sell Lisa Marsh as a sex slave to your friends?"

"What the fuck is this?" He raised his voice.

"Just answer the fucking question!" Nick interrupted.

"Did you sell Lisa Marsh as a sex slave to your friends?" Martha continued.

"No!"

"Do you know who killed Scotty Branning?"

"No."

"Is water your favourite drink?"

"No."

"Do you know who killed Lisa Marsh?"

"No."

"Did you sell Lisa to Scotty Branning?"

"Yes."

"Did you sell Lisa to John McKennith?"

"No."

"Is green your favourite colour?"

"Yes."

"Do you own a car?"

"No."

"Do you know what happened to Scotty Branning?"

"No."

"Did you threaten 6 women to pull their accusations of rape against Scotty Branning so he didn't have to face jail?"

"No, I didn't. I'm done. I'm done with this shit!" He pulled the pulse reader off his finger, ripped off the blood pressure band and yanked at the chest piece that Michael ended up detaching for him.

"Guard!" Nick called. A tall man entered the room, big and bulky with muscles. "Take him to a holding cell. We're done here."

"I'll get the results to you ASAP," Michael promised.

* * *

"While we wait for the results, I think it's about time we pay this John McKennith a visit," Nick suggested to Martha.

"I couldn't agree more." The two detectives headed towards Nick's Mazda and within 10 minutes found themselves outside of John's house. Martha rang on the doorbell, then shivered. It had started to snow once again, but the ground was too wet to allow it to settle.

A few seconds later, an old woman, probably about 62, answered the door. "Yes?" She said through the crack of the door, refusing to open it wide, leaving the chain lock in place.

"I'm Detective Willis, and this is my partner Detective Hardy. We're looking for a Mr John McKennith?"

"I'm Judy McKennith. John is my son. What has he got himself into this time?" She turned her back on the two detectives and began to yell in the direction of the stairs within her house. "JOHN! Two police are here to see you!" She turned back to face the detectives once again. "Please, come in." She gestured toward the living room.

After about 5 minutes of waiting, John finally entered the living room. He was a lot smaller than Martha was expecting. No muscles, and very thin. His hair was blonde and thinning, making him look a lot older than his actual age of 32.

"Yes?" He grunted as he sat down in the armchair next to the detectives.

"We're working on a murder case involving Lisa Marsh. It has been reported that you were one of the last people to have seen her alive." Nick stated.

"BOLLOCKS!" He yelled. "I don't even know a fucking Lisa!"

"You're lying through your teeth!"

"And how'd you figure that out?"

"Your semen was found on and inside of Lisa Marsh's vagina. That suggests you're a liar and that you raped her along with your friend Scotty Branning!" Martha snapped.

"Look, right! I didn't mean to!"

"Did you kill her?"

"No! I mean, we tackled her to the ground while she tried to escape, but we never killed her!"

"But you admit to raping her?"

"I paid for it, so yes! There was no way I was letting her go without getting what I paid for!"

"She had cancer, for fuck's sake!"

"Well then, she didn't have long left anyway, might as well make the most of what you've got, aye?"

"You have no remorse?"

"It was a business transaction. Jason was paid in cash, in full. I was getting my end no matter what." He smirked.

"Jason says you weren't allowed to have Lisa, so how could you pay him in full for something he wasn't selling to you?"

"Right, you got me. I paid Scotty instead. I knew Jason wouldn't let me have Lisa, so I paid Scotty to share her during the time he had purchased her, without Jason knowing, okay?"

"And then you killed her?" Nick pressed on.

"I already said I didn't kill her. I'm not a fucking murderer."

"No? Just a sick and twisted rapist, huh?"

John's only reply was a grunt. His mother wasn't in the room, and that was probably a good thing, to save her from hearing such horrors coming from her own son's mouth.

"You saw Lisa alive last, so who killed her?"

"I don't know! Scotty and I left her alive."

"And how do you know she was alive?"

"Because she was crying like a little bitch! We left her with some chick."

"Who?" Mather asked.

"Dunno her name, but she's been hanging around Jason for some time. Think they're fuck buddies, to be honest."

"Did she have earrings?"

"Only one, why?"

"Investigative purposes."

"John McKennith, I am arresting you for the rape of Lisa Marsh. You do not have to say anything, but it may harm your defence if you do not mention when questioned something which you may later rely on in court. Anything you do say may be given in evidence." Nick pulled John up from his chair, placed his arms around his back, and cuffed him all in a matter of seconds.

CHAPTER TWENTY-SIX

"**So, we have two suspects in custody,** and neither is admitting to murdering Lisa. John McKennith has admitted to raping her, and if justice is served rightly, he'll spend the next 30 years behind bars. Jason on the other hand, I don't think any of us knows where that investigation is going." Nick complained, staring at his computer screen.

"Never mind that, one of the 6 girls has just emailed me."

"What? Which one? What did she say?" He got out of his chair at speed and rushed round to Martha and began looking at her screen.

"Nadia Pugh, councillor for victims of rape:

"*Evening, Detective Martha Willis. I am willing to work with your team involving my historic rape case and hope to help bring justice to Lisa Marsh. I have been watching the news lately and it has brought everything back up to the surface. I tell my classes to stand tall and fight back, how can I preach and not practice? It is my turn now. My story is ready to be told. I am willing to meet up tomorrow morning at the MSMI Bureau, for I cannot attend at the Police Station due to the fear of seeing Jason who is currently being held there. I hope this is okay, and that I hear from you again soon. Thank you, Nadia Pugh.*"

"What do you reckon?" Nick asked.

"I'll meet with her tomorrow. I'll book out a small room so we can talk in private and confidentially. I think you should continue working on Jason and John down at the Police Station while Nadia and I talk."

"I understand. You'll be okay?"

"Always."

* * *

It was now Saturday the 25th of February, 35 days after Lisa's body was found. Martha found herself sitting in a small room with Nadia Pugh. Two armchairs were all that occupied the space, the walls were cream and the floor was newly laminated, yet the room was still rather lacklustre. Nadia pulled her black hair away from her face and tied what little of the shoulder-length cut back into a short ponytail. Her hands were trembling and sweating, her left leg bouncing continually due to her anxiety, and maybe a touch of alcohol withdrawal; at least that was what Martha could garner from the situation, given the information on the NCLB Database about Nadia's continual struggles with alcohol since her rape ordeal. Martha offered her a glass of water to help keep her mouth lubricated and hopefully help with the anxiety. She accepted gracefully and forced a small smile to say thank you.

"We'll do this in your own time. If you don't want to talk just yet, that's fine. I will wait until you're ready and comfortable." Martha explained.

"Thank you." She said quietly. "It was about 7 years ago when I met Scot Guilds, though the news says he is now known as Scotty Branning. I knew it was him the second they showed his photo." She paused and took a sip of her water. "I was out partying with my friends. I drunk a lot that night, and I mean a lot. I remember dancing with him. We tried talking but it was just too loud, so we went outside for a cigarette and some conversation time. He was funny. I was so drawn into him that I didn't realise that my friends were no longer around. They moved onto the next club and I had no idea. There I was, half-cut, talking to a stranger, all on my own. He offered me this pill, said it was Ecstasy. I was young, stupid, drunk, and looking for a good time. So I took it. Needless to say, it wasn't Ecstasy at all, but rather some kind of date rape drug that pretty much paralysed me. I was aware of everything around me, but I couldn't move. I even struggled to blink. Next thing I knew I was in some cheap motel room, completely naked, and there he was, on top of me, inside me. I tried to scream but my lips wouldn't move, my vocal cords wouldn't work. I was completely paralysed. All I managed was silent tears. He wiped them away and said "Don't cry. You'll enjoy it. Trust me!" And so I just shut my eyes, tried to imagine myself somewhere else. But I couldn't. I just lay there thinking, *knowing,* that it was all my fault!" Tears began to stream down her face.

"No, Nadia. If there is one thing I know for certain, it's that it was *not* your fault!"

"But it was though. I didn't drink sensibly, and I took a tablet off a stranger. I thought I was all cool."

"You were only 20! You did what all young men and women do!"

"I knew better, though. My mum always rammed it into my head. *"Don't talk to strangers. Don't do drugs."* I couldn't have gotten it any more wrong than I did that night." She took another sip of her water and dried her tears with some tissue that Martha had given her. "Anyway, when the drug finally wore off, Scot was gone. It was just me in the motel room. I called the police instantly, bawling my eyes out. They took swabs, any evidence from the motel room and even sought after the CCTV. I was adamant that I would get him put away, to stop him from doing this to any other women. I wanted to make that difference. But then, just a few days later, this man called Jason Stark was at my doorstep, middle of the night, with a gun to my head. Another mistake of mine, answering to a complete stranger at stupid o'clock in the morning."

"You wasn't to know."

"Well, I wish I did. He said, *"You withdraw your complaint against Scot, tell them you got it wrong, or I will kill your family, your beloved pets, and then I will kill you!"* My heart was racing faster than ever before. I felt physically sick, my body trembling. Needless to say, I withdrew my complaint, said it was consensual sex and that the only reason why I reported it in the first place was because I was ashamed and embarrassed about having a one-night-stand. It couldn't have been any further from the truth, but they accepted it none-the-less."

"I'm so sorry you had to go through all of that." Deep inside, Martha just wanted to curl up and cry. Cry for herself, and cry for the 6 women who had their lives stolen from them. But she remained collected and professional. "Do you know the other 5 victims?"

"I know *of* them. Rumours went around about women being threatened at gunpoint in order to save a serial rapist. Everyone thought it was just some sick joke to scare the women into staying at home rather than partying with friends. But I knew it was true, and I couldn't say anything about it without fear of killing my parents. There is one thing I want to know, though."

"What's that?"

"How does my case help Lisa's?"

"We don't know who killed Lisa yet, but we know Scot Guilds raped her before she died. And shortly after, Scot Guilds was also murdered."

"Karma."

"Indeed. But we have to find his killer."

"Why? The killer did us all a favour."

"Maybe, but maybe the killer was also Lisa's killer. Maybe other women are in trouble while the killer is loose. We honestly don't know what could happen if the killer isn't caught. But Jason knows something, and he is the one who threatened you and the other 5 girls all those years ago. He is linked to this entire case, and it coincides with your case, too.

If you testify against him, we can put him behind bars for even longer than what we could if we didn't have you to testify. Jason somehow kidnapped Lisa and sold her on to his friends as a sex slave, and one of those friends was Scot Guilds, except he committed the crime under his new alias. It all links together, and with your help, we can re-open your case and make him pay for the evil he has done. But that's entirely up to you, and I do not want to force you into anything, especially if you're not ready."

"No, I'm ready. It's been 7 years. I may not get to see justice hit Scot, but at the very least I can get justice against the mastermind himself, and stop him from hurting anyone else ever again!"

CHAPTER TWENTY-SEVEN

The weekend seemed to drag on for Martha and Nick. The wait for the lie detector results was excruciating. What could they possibly uncover from the results? How much of the truth was Jason telling them? Martha ran Nick through the meeting she had with Nadia, and he agreed things were starting to look positive, what with Nadia's report looking to promise a long sentence for Jason, whatever the outcome of Lisa Marsh's case would be.

It was almost time for bed, but Martha decided to try and get hold of Tyler once again, desperate to find out where she was and that she was okay.

"Hey, it's Tyler. I can't get to the phone just yet, so leave a message and I'll call you back!" Her soft and bubbly voice instructed.

"Hey, Tyler, it's me again. Call me when you can. I'm starting to worry now. Lots of love!"

"Have you tried her husbands' number?"

"I don't have it. Ugh! Honestly, this is really getting to me now. Where is she?"

"Look, she'll be okay. Give it one more day and if you still don't hear from her or her husband then we will make a report and go out and search for her. But I'm sure it won't come to that. She might have lost her phone and is too busy to pop round. Not to mention we're at work most hours of the day. Just calm down."

"I'll try. I just hope she and baby are okay."

Nick pulled her into a hug. "They'll both be okay. Now, we have work in the morning and hopefully the lie detector results, so get some rest and we will revisit this in the morning, okay?"

"Yeah, okay." She pulled out of the hug and headed to her bedroom. "Goodnight, Nick."

"Nunnight Martha."

* * *

Monday the 27th of February, day 37 in Lisa Marsh's case. Michael Lance kept to his promise and rushed the lie detector test results.

"Well, looks like Jason wasn't telling us the full truth after all, and he is going to regret that," Nick stated. "A deal is a deal, and he broke it."

The two detectives walked into interrogation room 2 where Jason was currently waiting.

"Well?" He asked.

"The results are in, and they're rather interesting," Martha claimed. "We'll go through the important ones together. So, were you involved in the kidnapping of Lisa Marsh? You said yes, and you were telling the truth."

"Obviously! I already told you that."

"Yes, but it gets better. Did you deal drugs to Scotty Branning?"

"No."

"Liar!" Nick slammed his fist on the table, his voice echoing in the small space.

"Fuck off!"

"Why did you lie?"

"I can't be arsed with this shit."

"Well suck it up buttercup because there is more where that came from!"

"Did you sell Lisa Marsh as a sex slave to your friends? You said no, and that was also a lie!" Martha continued to read off the results.

"I needed the cash! I was desperate. She let me do it!"

"And I suppose she let you tie her up while her body was being abused, too, huh? Next question: Do you know who killed Scotty Branning. You said no. That was a lie. Do you know who killed Lisa Marsh? You said no, and that was a fucking lie too! And the last one, did you threaten 6 women to pull their accusations of rape against Scotty Branning so he didn't have to face jail? You said no, and that was a big fat fucking lie! You held a gun to their heads and threatened their families so a rapist could go free. Why?"

"I don't have to listen to any of this!"

"Oh, but you do. When we made that deal, you waived your rights to a lawyer. And stupid little you decided to go back on the deal and lie through your teeth. You will not be staying in an open prison, but rather a high-security one instead."

"That's not fucking fair!" He yelled.

"Well neither was holding your cancer-ridden girlfriend hostage, but you did it anyway!" Martha snapped.

"She had cancer?" He began to smirk.

"What are you smirking at?" Nick snarled.

"She was dying anyway. I made her last two weeks on Earth unforgettable. She enjoyed every minute. We made the most of the situation. She only would have died alone and bald otherwise. Funny how things work out, huh?"

"There is fuck all funny about that!" The fury in Nick's voice was undeniable. Martha could tell from the look on his face that he just wanted to shoot Jason right between his eyes, but he couldn't, and it was a hard fight against such a strong and understandable urge.

"What happened to Scotty?" Martha intercepted, trying to cool the atmosphere but desperately trying to get answers at the same time.

"He fucked up my income, okay?"

"What do you mean?"

"Lisa was my main source of income. I let Scotty pay for a turn. I left like I did every other time, and went to the pub. Scotty thought it would be a bright idea to untie Lisa, the fucking idiot. I come back the next day and she's gone. Next thing I know she's all over the fucking news as being murdered. I tracked him down to his apartment and there he was without a care in the world getting high off his fucking face. He denied killing her and slipped up saying John didn't kill her either. I didn't even get payment from him, but there he was fucking her, too. I lost my temper, filled a syringe with a lethal amount of meth, and stabbed him right in the arm. Made it look like a suicide. But you brats already figured that out didn't you?" He sat back, sighed in relief, and smirked.

Why is he smiling? We've literally got him bang to rights! He must be delusional.

"What makes you think Scotty was the murderer?"

"Because he was the last person I sold her to, and that very night she goes missing and gets killed. It's not fucking rocket science."

"What about John?" Nick asked.

"I don't know where that prick is, but he owes me my fucking cash!"

"Cash that you can't spend in prison."

"Who's the other woman?" Martha asked.

"Huh?"

"The other woman who helped you abuse Lisa."

"And what makes you think I had another woman there?"

"We found an earring on the floor, right by the chair Lisa was tied to."

"Well then, it was obviously Lisa's, huh."

"She didn't have any piercings."

"Then it's a coincidence."

"No, you're still not telling us the whole truth! Who was she?"

"I'm getting fuck all out of this except a longer sentence every time I give you info, so you can fucking do one and find out yourselves. After all, you are detectives. How good are you at detecting?"

* * *

"So, we have who killed Scotty, how and why. We know Jason was involved in kidnapping Lisa, and that he held her hostage and sold her on for sex, but we have no idea who killed her, and who actually pulled off the kidnapping while allowing Jason to work on his alibi. It leaves us with John McKennith, and then this mysterious woman who just so happened to lose her earring at the scene of the crime, covered in blood. But who's blood? We'll have to chase that up with Jessica." Martha deducted. "Have I missed anything?"

"Just the fact that Jason is going to prison for a very long time. Have we heard from any of Scotty and Jason's previous victims?"

"Nothing as of yet, but Nadia is still adamant she wants to take this to court and bring him down. So yes, he will be behind bars for years to come. I'm intrigued though."

"About what?"

"Well, Jason is adamant that Scotty was Lisa's murderer, and that's why he killed him. But hearing from John, it seems that they both left her alive after raping her. That leaves only this mystery woman, the owner of the earring, to be the one who killed her."

"But Jason answered the lie detector saying he knew who killed Lisa, and he told us it was Scotty, and the test results said that was the truth?" Nick questioned.

"No. The test results show he was telling the truth about knowing who killed Lisa because in his mind he *knows* it's Scotty. He has no reason to believe it was anyone else. That means he was telling *his* truth. The actual truth, however, was that Scotty and John left her alive and crying after raping her, and left her in the hands of some woman who had been hanging around with Jason, so they had no reason to doubt she wouldn't care for Lisa, let alone become her murderer. Who is this woman, and why did she kill Lisa? Jason seems very fond and protective over her, though I doubt he will feel that way when he finds out his precious bit on the side was his 'incomes' killer. We need to track her down ASAP."

* * *

Jason and John remained in custody, while Lisa and Scotty lay in the Forensics Lab with Jessica looking into the lead-up to their deaths, as well as finalising the results on the blood of the earring.

"What have you got for us, Jessica?" Martha asked, taking a seat on a swivel chair, Nick joining her.

"I can confirm that Lisa's death resulted in continuous impact upon a hard surface, at least half a dozen times until she lost consciousness. The loss of blood resulted in her death mere minutes after the brutal attack. It would have been extremely painful for her. The lack of depth in the wound suggests it was done by a woman, someone naturally weaker than a man. The repetitiveness of the assault caused the most damage and her untimely death, as opposed to the strength used. There was also skin under her fingernails that didn't match her own DNA, but rather that of another person."

"Scotty or John?"

"Neither."

"Then who?"

"Unfortunately we do not have a match on our database, but it is indeed a match for the blood and traces of skin found on the earring."

"So that means?"

"Yes, the mysterious woman who helped Jason sell Lisa for sex was the perpetrator who went on to brutally murdering her, shortly after being raped twice in a cold, dark, and damp alleyway."

"That's horrific!" Nick sighed, the thought of what Lisa must have suffered running through his head at a million miles.

"So we know who killed Lisa, but we don't have her identity. The only one who knows who she is is Jason."

"He won't tell us in a million years!" Martha remarked.

"Maybe not, but if we can get a warrant for his flat, maybe we can find some evidence like photos or something that would give the game up and result in another confession and the woman's arrest!"

"Yes!" Martha yelped with confidence. "There's got to be evidence somewhere. Jason doesn't have enough brain cells to hide the master-mind behind all of this!"

CHAPTER TWENTY-EIGHT

Martha and Nick sat in their office awaiting confirmation of a warrant to search Jason's house and all of his belongings. Whilst waiting, a disturbance began in the foyer, just outside their office door.

"I need to see Martha! It's urgent!" A male voice called out.

"Well, you can't! You need to calm down right now!" A female replied, Taz.

"My wife is missing and you want me to fucking calm down? She's pregnant for fuck's sake!"

"Hey, hey! I'm here." Martha called out whilst opening her office door. "Derek Kin, please, calm down and come into my office." Her voice was calm and soft, but inside she was trembling with fear. *Where's Tyler?!*

They both went into the office and took a seat at the desk. Nick, looking concerned, wheeled his chair over to join them.

"Right, slowly tell me what's going on," Martha instructed.

"Tyler, she hasn't been home all weekend. I thought maybe she was with you. I tried calling her to confirm that but it just kept going straight to voicemail, and I don't have your number. I thought I'd give her benefit of the doubt until this morning. I was cleaning the living room when I found Tyler's phone lodged down the side of the sofa. The battery was completely dead. I charged it up and saw that you had missed called her.

I played the voicemails and that's when I realised she wasn't with you either. Then I came straight here. I didn't know what else to do!" He started bawling his eyes out. "My wife and my unborn baby are missing and I don't know what to do!" He was almost howling by this point. The pain was real and deep. Martha moved around to him and gave him a tight hug whilst looking over his shoulder at Nick. She looked terrified, and Nick could see that from a mile off.

"You did the right thing, coming straight to us!" Martha said in his ear and then pulled back from the hug.

"We'll put a search party out ASAP," Nick put his hand on Derek's shoulder. "We'll find her, I promise."

"What do you think's happened?" He sobbed.

"I don't know. But we will check with all local hospitals to see if she has been admitted anywhere. That will be the best place for us to start, with the off chance that she may have had an accident and the hospital staff not knowing who to call due to the absence of her phone."

"So she could be unconscious in a hospital somewhere, and my unborn baby?"

"He didn't say that," Martha interrupted. "It's just a precaution. We have to stay positive. We'll phone all our friends and see if anyone knows anything. In the meantime, we have to remain calm. Can you do that for me?"

"Yes, I will try. Thank you!"

"Good, now get yourself home."

"But I want to help."

"You will be helping. For all we know she could walk through your front door at any moment. We're going to need you there in case she does."

* * *

"I knew something was wrong when she wasn't answering her calls," Martha told Nick.

"I'm sorry I ignored your worries."

"No, it's not your fault. You weren't to know, you were just trying to help."

"So when was the last time you saw her officially?"

"I last saw her when she left yours for the spa treatment I had organised for the day. That was exactly a week ago. Haven't heard from her since."

"And what about Derek?"

"Saturday morning. She told him she had some baby errands to run. He offered to go with her but work called him in saying he was needed desperately, so she went baby shopping alone."

"What's his job?"

"Security. He usually only works on weekdays but this one time the person who was meant to be in called in sick, so Derek agreed to stand in and get extra pay to put towards the baby. She'll be 18 weeks tomorrow. Her baby scan is due in the next 4 weeks." Martha paused to take a breath as a single tear slid down the side of her cold cheek.

Nick then wiped it away with his thumb and proceeded to hug her. "We'll find her soon. Everyone is out looking for her. Who knows, Derek might call in a bit saying she's come home and she was just at another mate's house and couldn't call due to misplacing her phone."

"I hope you're right. I don't know what I'd do if anything bad happens to her. She's been my friend since Primary School."

"I know. I'm going to be with you in this, every step of the way."

A knock at the office door, then Mohammad walked in with a piece of paper. "Here you go, your warrant to search Jason's home and belongings." He handed it over to Nick. "Oh, and Martha, I hope your friend is found soon. If you need anything, let me know." Before Martha could thank him, he was already walking out of the door and leaving the foyer.

"Do you want to stay here?" Nick asked.

"No. I need to keep busy. I'll come. Let's nail this son of a bitch together!"

CHAPTER TWENTY-NINE

Martha and Nick were in Jason's flat sifting through all of his stuff along with a team of forensics.

"Martha, Nick!" Jessica called from the bedroom.

"What's up?" Nick answered as they both walked into the room.

"I have taken swabs from Jason's bed. There seems to be evidence of bodily fluids on the sheets. I can guarantee none of it will belong to his actual girlfriend, as it outdates her death."

"Another one night stand?"

"That, or the mysterious woman he has been hanging around with." Martha interrupted.

"Very true. Anything else, Jessica?"

"Not as of yet, but I believe Michael may have found something on Jason's computer."

The two detectives went over to the computer desk in which Michael was working on. "Anything?" Nick asked.

"This lot are obsessed with porn! That's all I've seen in this case. Porn here, porn there!"

"Michael, focus!"

"Yes, of course! He's been messaging some woman on a dating site called LoveLess, MoreSex."

"Do we have a name?" Martha asked.

"Unfortunately she is only known as LB.abe."

"What kind of name is that?" Nick said.

"Any pictures?"

"Just a close up of her tits, which, in my honest opinion, are extremely disappointing."

"Okay. So we're in the search for a mystery woman who goes by the alias LB.abe and has rubbish tits. Great." Martha replied sarcastically. "Do we know if she is our woman?"

"I believe so. Going by their chats, they have definitely met and have most definitely done the deed."

"What deed?" Nick asked, resulting in a snigger from Martha. "What?" He repeated.

"They've had sex!" Martha snorted. "Honestly, have you never heard of the saying, "done the deed"?"

"Nope, never."

"Well, you learn something new every day, huh?" Martha smirked. *Bless him, so innocent.*

"How do we know they did the '*deed*', then?" He asked.

"Their messages about how great it felt and that she should come round his more often. They also talk about being a great team, selling sex for money, though he refuses to become an item with her because of 'priorities'."

"I assume they're talking about Lisa?"

"Most definitely, it would certainly make sense."

"Can we find her IP Address?" Martha asked.

"Yup, but I'm going to need more time."

"That's fine, Michael. Thank you." Nick said.

* * *

It had been a long and excruciating day for the detectives, what with the lie detector results, the search of Jason's apartment, and the news of Martha's best friend Tyler going missing. It felt like a week all rolled into one, leaving Martha and Nick with little energy to even cook themselves dinner.

"Takeaway?" Martha asked.

"Ooo, yes!"

"Chinese?"

"You're speaking my language." They were sat in Martha's living room, and as promised, Nick was staying another night to make sure she felt safe and guarded. He even organised a watch team to keep an eye on the apartment and surrounding areas.

He is such a gentleman. How could I ever repay him for everything he has done for me?

No news came about Tyler's disappearance, so Nick encouraged the "no news is good news" motto, otherwise he knew she would not sleep, which would be detrimental to her health and work for the next day.

CHAPTER THIRTY

I t had now been 44 days since Lisa's body was found, and 7 days since Derek reported Tyler as missing. By this point, Martha was almost ready to pull her hair out. *We have no leads as to where Tyler is, nothing useful was found in Jason's flat, as the bodily fluids were simply that of a well-known prostitute that gave no leads, and the killer is still on the loose! Even the IP addresses came up with nothing. How was that even possible? Michael has been wracking his brain about it for days, losing out on sleep. This is ridiculous.*

"What are you thinking?" Nick asked, with his legs perched upon his desk while he chewed on the end of his pen.

"I'm thinking, how the hell can Jason keep shtum on who the woman is, knowing full well she could be the killer of his main 'income'? How has he not cracked under the pressure? He has been locked in a cell for a week and we have nothing! And it's been the same length of time since finding out that Tyler has gone missing, and once again we have NOTHING! I'm left thinking how much of a pathetic detective I am!"

"I'm a pathetic detective?"

"What? No! I said I am!"

"But we work together, as a team, and I have no leads on either case, so I'm in the same boat as you. If you're pathetic, then so am I!"

"You're far from it."

"Then stop beating yourself up! Until we get something, it's hardly our fault how much time passes. We're working as hard as we can, and that's all anyone asks for. Dedication. Pure dedication and that's what you have, and that makes you a *good* detective!"

Martha let out a smirk, "Thanks." A frown crossed her face, serious.

"Martha?" Nick asked, but he received no reply. "Hey! Earth to Martha! What's up?"

"Why didn't we think of this before?!" She yelped, jumping out of her chair.

"What?"

"We are stupid detectives! Real fucking stupid detectives!"

"Why? What is it!"

"John, he raped Lisa and said he left her alive with some woman who had been hanging around Jason a lot, possibly even having sex together." She began.

"Yes, I know that. Your point?"

"If we can get a sketch artist in, John can tell us what she looked like and maybe with the final picture we can put it on the news for people who recognise her to come forward."

"Martha Willis, I think you may have just cracked the case! But how are we going to get John to sing?"

"We'll have to make a deal worth his while."

"Like what?"

"I think I might have just the thing!" She winked, and then left their office, Nick hurrying after her.

* * *

"If you don't cooperate, Jason and you will be in the same prison. He already knows you raped Lisa, though he claims he never allowed that to happen. And he is 100% set on you being the murderer!" Martha explained.

"But I didn't kill her! You have to tell him that!"

"We have, and he refuses to believe us. He is out for your blood, John."

"There must be something you can do! I don't want to die! I can't be in the same prison as him! I can't!"

"There is something we can do, but we'll need your help."

"What is it? Anything, just please keep that psycho away from me!"

"We will make sure you go to a different prison to Jason, and we will appeal for a lesser sentence *if* you talk to our sketch artist and work with him to produce an image of the woman that's been hanging around Jason recently."

"The one I left Lisa with?"

"Yes. Now, do we have a deal?"

"Yes! Absolutely, yes!"

* * *

The sketch artist, Dom, was sat in the interrogation room opposite John. Martha and Nick watched on from the observation room, listening to every word.

"She was blonde, from root to tip. Shoulder length, beautiful. She was stunning. Her eyes were like crystal blue in the sunlight. She wore little makeup, very natural. She had faded freckles spread evenly across her cheeks and her nose. She stood tall, about 6ft. Though she might have been wearing heels, she still had a stern tall, beautiful figure. She was authoritative, with faint lines across her forehead. I'd say she was probably in her early 30s. She was quite pale, but the blonde of her hair complimented her skin. Her nose was thin and her lips had a natural pout to them. Irresistible. She had a side fringe and a middle parting, and a beauty spot just above her lip on the left side. Her left. She wore a diamond earring, both ears were pierced but the left piercing was not there."

"Oh my god!" Martha shuddered.

"What? What is it?" Nick asked.

"I think I know who she is!"

"What? How? Who?"

"No. I'm going to wait for the sketch." Her body was trembling. *It can't be. Surely!*

* * *

Dom finally left the interrogation room with a sketch in his hands, John waiting patiently behind.

"Let us see," Martha ordered. Dom handed the sketch over, and Martha's breath got caught in her throat.

"But that's!" Nick began.

"Yes, I know."

"Leanne Baker! Also known as LB.abe."

"The woman who 'found' the body. It was her all along!"

CHAPTER THIRTY-ONE

Leanne Baker found herself in interrogation room 3, Martha and Nick sitting opposite her.

"Look, I honestly don't know why I'm here. I've told you everything I know!" She frowned.

"Not everything, Miss Baker," Nick said.

"Well go on then! What haven't I told you!"

"That you've been sleeping with the victim's boyfriend. That you helped hold her hostage and sell her for sex. That she pulled out one of your earrings as you was untying her so Scotty and John could have their fill, and that's why your ear has a cut on it. She did that! And after she was raped in a back alley, you killed her. But why? She was your lovers' income. He would kill you if he knew you were the true murderer. Instead, you played him, and you played us into thinking it was Scotty and John who killed her. You made out to everyone that you found the body, and that you had no idea who she was. You played us pretty well!"

"None of that is true! I've never seen her before in my life. I've never met Jason, Scotty, or John!"

"How do you know about Jason, then?" Martha quizzed.

"Because you said he was Lisa's boyfriend."

"No, we didn't. We just said boyfriend and lover, we never gave him a name. So, I'll ask you again; how do you know about Jason?"

"I want a lawyer!"

"Be our guest, but they won't be able to get you out of this one!" Martha smirked. *We got you, bitch!*

* * *

Leanne spent the next hour talking to her lawyer, trying to figure a way out of the mess she had just dug herself into. Jessica's group of Forensic Scientists spent this time searching Leanne's house, focusing mainly on the kitchen. Martha's phone began to ring.

"Martha speaking," she said.

"Hello, Martha," Jessica replied. "We have found a blunt kitchen knife that matches the weapon that was used to assault Lisa Marsh. UV Light has revealed some specks of blood that has not been cleaned properly, and I have a hunch it will be a match to our victim. We have even found some clothes shoved behind the wardrobe in the main bedroom, covered in bloodstains. We will get it to the lab ASAP, but I am almost certain that the blood will also be a match to Lisa's."

"Brilliant! Thank you, Jessica." She put the phone down. "We've got her, Nick. They've found the knife and blood-soaked clothes."

Finally, the lawyer gestured for Martha and Nick to come back in, and the interview was eventually resumed.

"Do you have anything that ties my client to the scene of the murder?"

"Yes, a willing and cooperative witness, and the knife that was used to assault our victim in the lead up to her murder, along with blood-soaked clothes hidden behind your client's wardrobe," Martha stated.

"And what about the place in which the victim was being held hostage?"

"Yes, we have what is believed to be Leanne Baker's earring."

"But is that certain?"

"It will be soon. The results are on their way to us thanks to our very capable forensics team." Nick said sternly, almost agitated.

"You see, this is going to go one way or the other. You either confess to aiding and abetting kidnapping and confess to murder, or we narrow down the evidence until we have means, motive, and opportunity that will stick in the court of law and send you down for years to come. So, Leanne, how do you want to play it?"

A knock at the door. A member of the Forensics' team walked in with a folder in their hands, containing the results on the blood test taken from the earring. Martha took the folder, read the document within, and nodded in a way to say *thank you, you can leave now.*

"What's that?" Leanne asked.

"This is the blood results that confirm that the blood and skin molecules found on the earring where Lisa was held hostage matches you down to the very last fibre! Not to mention the burnt remanence of the clothes found in the warehouse have been confirmed as Lisa's due to the remaining DNA particles left behind. It also turns out your own DNA is on her clothes, too. Funny that. I mean, if you didn't help kidnap her or play a part in her disappearance - meaning you never entered the warehouse - how did one of your earrings get there along with your DNA on Lisa's clothes? How was your DNA on her clothing when you claim you never met Lisa until finding her body? And why was your earring that was pulled out with force also found at the warehouse if you were never there?" Martha pressed.

"Look, right, I was doing her a favour! She was going to die sooner or later thanks to the torture Jason put her through. I simply ended her suffering. It was all down to Jason, and the arseholes who raped her!"

"Why don't you start from the beginning? Explain everything in as much detail, and we will see if you really 'did her a favour', hm?"

* * *

"Jason had been in a gang for as long as I have known him. Almost 10 years I would say. There was something about him that I admired. His masculinity, his superiority. He knew what he wanted and he would do anything to make sure he got it. I loved the bones of him but feared he would never love me back. When he went to protect his friend Scotty from being thrown in prison, I idolised him. He proved that he would always be there for the ones who supported him. One drunken night I opened up to him, told him how I felt. One thing led to another and we ended up having sex. It was powerful and full of emotions. He was very dominant and it was heavenly. The next morning he swore me to secrecy due to having a girlfriend, Lisa Marsh. I was so jealous, enraged even, but I made the promise none-the-less. A few weeks later he came to me about his money problems, that he was in debt with drug dealers all thanks to Scotty screwing the gang over. He was a heavy druggie. In the heat of the moment, my heart fluttering because he asked me for help, I just came up with the idea, and he loved it.

"We decided the best form of income was to sell Lisa for sex. We knew she would never agree to this, and I was far too loyal for Jason to turn on me. Him and Lisa were always fighting, so in his words, she 'had it coming'. On her way to work, on the 9th of January, I jumped her in the streets, using chloroform to bring her down easily, all while Jason got drunk at his local: a solid alibi. It was early morning so it was still dark. I managed to overpower her due to taking her by surprise, and I took her to a deserted warehouse and within the first couple of days, Jason had already made enough from her to pay back his debts. He was in love with the money, in love with the power he had over Lisa. He too would rape her, yet never glanced at me the same way. I was so annoyed. It was my idea, and yet to him, I was still some big mistake in the bedroom. All he wanted was her! The night of Lisa's death, Jason and I had a row. I told him I loved him and that I couldn't take being the side woman, the mistake, anymore! But he didn't care. He slapped me and put me in my place. He told me he was going to the local pub for the night, and that Scotty was coming round to have a go with Lisa, fully paid for. When John turned up with Scotty, I knew Jason would be furious that John hadn't paid, but I didn't care. This was my chance to get my own back. I asked Scotty how he would like to have his go without Lisa being tied down, and he thought it would be sexier. As I untied her, she head-butted me and pulled out my earring, causing my ear to bleed. I went to slap her but she pushed past me and the lads. I screamed at them to catch her, otherwise, Jason would kill us all. She would go straight to the police and report us, and Jason would go out of his way to make sure I paid for this mistake.

"Anyway, the lads caught up to her by the time we reached the alley she was found in. They jumped her, causing her to hit her head on the pavement. Scotty refused to take her back to the warehouse because he had paid for her, and he wanted what he paid for. Helping me bring her back to her prison wasn't part of the deal. He raped her, and soon after, so did John. They both left after, laughing, while Lisa lay there naked, bleeding and crying. I tried to feel sorry for her until I remembered how much Jason cared for her and not me. The rage took over, and that's when I attacked her."

* * *

"You bitch! You selfish, selfish bitch!" Leanne screamed as she grabbed a hand full of Lisa's hair.

"Get off me! Please, get off!" She sobbed. The pain was real and intense.

Her vagina bled uncontrollably, the back of her head was throbbing, her ribs burning. "Please, I'm sorry! I will do anything! Just please, let me go! I won't tell anybody!" By this point, she knew she was pleading for her life.

"No! You stole Jason! I'm meant to be his lover, not you! You're a fucking selfish little slag!" She clenched her hand tighter around Lisa's hair and then shoved her head down with force onto the pavement. Within the first hit, she could hear and even feel Lisa's skull crack. Lisa let out a scream of agony. But this wasn't enough for Leanne. Concealed in her pocket was a kitchen knife taken from her home. Since meeting Jason, it was something that she found she could no longer leave the house without. In a fit of rage, she brought the knife down towards Lisa's face. Lisa threw her hands in the air and grabbed hold of the blade, cutting deep into her palm. She was slashed again on the other palm and multiple times over her arms as she begged for the attack to stop.

Leanne threw the knife to her side, grabbed hold of Lisa's hair once more and smashed her head into the ground again! "You are a waste of life! No one cares about you! It's been two weeks since you went missing and no one has come looking! You're dead to everyone already! And you'll be dead to me too!" She smashed her head one last time, but nothing escaped Lisa's lips. Leanne released her grip and Lisa fell limply to the ground. "Lisa?" She asked softly, stunned. She took two fingers to Lisa's neck and checked her pulse. Nothing. She put her head to Lisa's mouth to listen for breathing and stared at her naked chest to see if it would rise and fall. Nothing. "Oh shit!" She whispered. She couldn't believe she had done it. She had actually killed someone. "Fuck, fuck, fuck!! Jason will kill me!" She tried to suppress the bleeding on Lisa's hands, and then the back of her head, but nothing would stop the blood flow. She tried CPR in a panic, but it was too little too late; nothing would bring Lisa back. She sat on the wet pavement, her left ear bleeding, her hand pulsating from the beating she just gave Lisa, the naked woman who lay lifeless and bloody by her side, cuts and bruises covering her, even infected ones. "Scotty. It has to be Scotty."

* * *

"Scotty?" Martha asked.

"Yes. Jason knew he was the last person to pay for Lisa, and the last person to see her alive, so I framed him. I had no choice if I wanted to live. I pretended I had found the body so I could keep in the loop of the investigation. When no one could track down Scotty's involvement thanks to the rape cases that got him a new identity, I knew I had to insert the idea of his involvement myself, hence my visit to the MSMI Bureau. Jason had no idea that I 'found' the body, or that I had any connection to the investigation, which made things a lot easier, because he would then have no need to bring me up to the police, and no need to kill me. As soon as he found out about Scotty's apparent involvement in Lisa's death, he wanted to get to him before you did. Thankfully Scotty was a druggie, so it was pretty easy staging his death as an overdose."

"You helped kill Scotty?" Nick asked in disbelief.

"Yes, I had to. I had to do everything Jason told me otherwise I was dead. And I couldn't chance him finding out I had let Lisa go and then proceeded to kill her, so I had to play along with the charade to save my own skin. At least Scotty died due to something he loved."

"Oh, so that makes it all better, does it?" Martha said sarcastically.

"Obviously not, but I had no choice if I wanted to live!"

"You could have come clean the moment Jason began torturing Lisa!"

"No, I couldn't."

"Why?" Nick asked.

"Because I loved him, and I would do anything for him!"

"But you're scared of him yourself!"

"It just adds that extra dimension. The fear, never knowing what to expect. It's exciting. That's what I fell for."

"You're completely delusional," Nick said.

"What did Jason say about your ear? Surely he noticed your ear was ripped open?" Martha added.

"He didn't take any notice. Unfortunately, he doesn't feel for me the way I feel for him, meaning any cuts or bruises I have simply go unnoticed."

"So why are you coming clean about it all now?"

"My lawyer advised me to tell the truth," her lawyer gave a nod. "And by telling the truth, you guys have to keep me away from Jason, to protect me. It was my safer option. So please, don't let him kill me!"

"One more question," Martha said.

"Yes?"

"How did you prevent us from tracking your LB.abe IP Address?"

"Jason did it for me. He set up a VPN for me so I was untraceable. I'm not very tech-savvy, I just know it did the job."

"You say Jason wouldn't acknowledge you, but the sex chats online prove otherwise. How can you explain that?" Nick added.

"We became what people call Friends with Benefits. That's all it was. Lisa was always number one."

"If that's how he treated his number one, I'd hate to see how he would treat his enemies!"

CHAPTER THIRTY-TWO

The detectives let a whole 24 hours pass in order to take in all the new information that they had received on Lisa's tragic murder. It was 10:05 am, and Martha and Nick were still in her apartment, having tea and toast in her kitchen. Martha had not long received a phone call from Jessica confirming that the blood-soaked clothes and burnt clothes matched with Lisa's DNA, along with the kitchen knife Leanne used to assault her.

"She played us all pretty well," Martha said glumly.

"But we've got her now! That's all that matters, and that's thanks to you!" Martha blushed but still felt like she didn't solve the case soon enough. "There's nothing more you could have done," he told her gently.

During their late breakfast, Nick received a text confirming Zahid Maul's fate. 1-year imprisonment for selling drugs and third-degree murder, manslaughter, eligible for parole in 6 months, and a £600 fine. With the help he offered the Detectives, his punishment was extremely lenient, though officers would be keeping a closer eye on him from now on.

* * *

Detectives Martha and Nick found themselves sitting opposite Jason once again.

"Leanne Baker," Nick said.

"Who?" Jason replied.

"The woman who gave you the idea to kidnap Lisa. The same woman you had sex with, and the same woman who let John rape Lisa against your instructions, and then proceeded to murder her."

"Who the fuck told you this?"

"Leanne Baker herself. She confessed, written and orally, and signed."

"That fucking slag! She killed Lisa?" He had no idea going by the puzzled look on his face, and the fresh burst of anger. "I fucking trusted her!"

"Is that why you refused to identify her?" Martha asked.

"Obviously!"

"You know that adds an extra charge of perverting the course of justice?"

"Like I give a fucking shit! My main source of income is dead and fucking buried, almost fucking literally! She was mine! She was a part of my possessions and now she is fucking gone!"

"So you remain adamant you were not involved in her murder?" Martha asked.

"100 fucking per cent. If I get my hands on that bitch I'll fucking kill her!"

"Good job you won't be seeing her again then, aye?" Nick said. "We look forward to seeing you in court, Jason." Both detectives got up and left the interrogation room, their work with Jason finally complete. It was now down to the lawyers, judge and jury to finish the rest.

* * *

Martha and Nick decided out of goodwill to pay Melanie and Hazel another visit.

"You did it! You really did it!" Melanie cried with happiness, hugging both of the detectives.

"Th-thank you so m-m-much!" Hazel sang their praise.

"Apparently the funeral is coming up next week?" Martha asked as they all sat down in the living room.

"Y-yes. Now that the MSMI have l-l-let the body go, we can f-finally put Lisa to r-r-rest."

"How are you both coping?"

"It's hard. It feels like an empty void not having Lisa around anymore." Melanie explained. "We've decided to join a charity that protects those who find themselves in an abusive relationship and helps them find shelter and protection. It helps us feel like we're making a change in Lisa's name, you know?"

"I know exactly what you mean, and it's lovely. What you're both doing is wonderful and will go on to help so many people. Thank you!"

"No, thank you for getting Lisa's killer!"

After catching up over the next 2 hours, it was finally time for Martha and Nick to leave and head back to work.

CHAPTER THIRTY-THREE

Nick was driving Martha and himself back to their office in the MSMI bureau when his phone began to ring.

"Detective Nick Hardy," he answered on the hands-free set.

"Hi, Nick. It's Mohammad Muskhan. We have news about Tyler Kin. We have a team in at Epping Forest. I suggest you and Detective Martha get out there ASAP." He ordered, not long before hanging up the phone, preventing the detectives from asking any questions.

Martha's heart began to race. *Oh no, this isn't good. Our boss called it in, in the fucking forest. Something bad has happened to her, I can feel it!*

It was about a half-hour drive from their location, and Martha felt physically sick the entire journey.

"It's okay, just try and stay calm. It could be anything!" Nick tried to reassure her, but he knew it wasn't working.

* * *

There was a small opening in the middle of the forest where a cabin sat in the cold shade, run down and covered in debris from the trees around it. Jessica and her forensics team were there in their white suits. *No. The forensic suits. This is not good*, Martha thought.

"Wait here," Nick told Martha, and then he headed inside the cabin. A few minutes passed before he came back out. Martha held her breath. "I'm sorry," he muttered, shaking his head.

"No! No, she can't!" Martha screamed and started toward the cabin.

"No, Martha!" Nick grabbed a hold of her and pulled her back. "You shouldn't!"

"I need to see her!"

"Not like this! You can't!"

"Yes, I fucking can!" She pulled her arm free from Nick's grip and ran into the cabin. Her eyes took a few seconds to adjust to the dark, and then she saw the room in full. Blood covered the walls and the floor, splattered around haphazardly, like a scene from a horror film. And there she was, Tyler Kin, Martha's best friend, lying lifeless up against a wall. Her face was black and blue, and a knife stood out from her chest, soaked in blood. Her once blue shirt was ripped open to reveal her belly. She had been completely cut open, her unborn baby half hanging out, the sack had been torn by the knife used to stab and cut Tyler open. The baby was lifeless, just like her mother. That poor, lifeless little girl, taken from the world before she even got to see it.

A lump filled in Martha's throat, her vision became blurry and dark, and she struggled to steady herself. Before she could react, she began to throw up, and soon after, darkness consumed her.

* * *

"She's dead. He murdered her? My stalker murdered my girl? My goddaughter?" Martha asked, more to herself than to Nick who sat there cradling his partner. "He wanted me to pay, to get revenge, so he killed my best friend and my goddaughter. It's all my fault, and I don't even know why. What did I do to this man to deserve this?" Her heart felt as though it was going to jump out of her chest and into a million pieces.

"You did nothing wrong! This is not your fault!"

"Yes, it is. Whatever I did to this man, if I didn't do it, then Tyler and her daughter would still be alive! She must have been terrified, and I was nowhere near to help save her." The tears were streaming uncontrollably, and there was nothing Nick could do or say that would help calm her down. He just had to let her work through the emotions.

"We'll get him. We will find him and we will make him pay, I promise!"

CHAPTER THIRTY-FOUR

A month had passed since the last interrogation took place with Jason, and since Tyler Kin was found brutally murdered in a cabin in the woods. It was Thursday the 13th of April, and Martha managed to bring herself into work for the first time since seeing her friend and goddaughter snatched from her life for good. She was told she could take more time off, but today was important. Today was the day that the verdicts would be announced involving the murder of Lisa Marsh.

The courtroom was spacious and airy, and light brown wood covered all of the furnishings. Leanne Baker, Jason Stark, and John McKennith were stood in a dock behind glass, security guards surrounding them. Leanne was crying, but the two men stood tall, Jason emotionless, John sweaty but confident. The jury was sat to the side of the room in view of everyone, and the judge was at her perch at the top of the room with an old white wig on her head. Martha sat next to Nick, hand in hand for support.

"Leanne Baker, on the counts of abduction and false imprisonment, human trafficking, perverting the course of justice and the murder of Lisa Marsh, and conspiring to murder Scotty Branning, formally known as Scot Guilds, you pleaded guilty. In this instance, I thank you for your eventual honesty, but I can still see the severity and sickness within such an awful case. You show remorse, yet I feel this may just be because you know you are about to lose your freedom. In regards to abduction or false imprisonment, you will receive a 10-year sentence. In addition to this, you will also receive 10 years for human trafficking, 12 years and eight months for murder, and finally 3 years for perverting the course of justice and 5 years for conspiring to murder. This tally's to a total of 40 years imprisonment, to run consecutively, no chance of parole. Take her down!"

Leanne burst into tears and screamed non-coherent words as the security guard by her side accompanied her out of the courtroom.

"John McKennith, on the counts of rape and assault, aiding and abetting, and perverting the course of justice, you pleaded guilty. For your eventual honesty, I must commend you, though the crimes you committed were severe. You have proven that you are a danger to women and cannot be trusted. For this, you will receive 3 years for GBH, 5 years for rape, 6 years for aiding and abetting, and 2 years for perverting the course of justice. This results in 16 years imprisonment, to run consecutively. No chance of parole. Take him down."

John let out a stifled sound but managed to hold back the tears that were fighting to come out. Within minutes, the guards led him out of the courtroom, and only Jason was left.

"Jason Stark, you are being charged with rape, assault, conspiring to kidnap and the human trafficking of Lisa Marsh. You are also being charged with the possession of Class A drugs, and for the murder of Scotty Branning, formally known as Scot Guilds. You pleaded not guilty to all charges. With the evidence presented to me, it is clear to see you are a compulsive liar and a danger to the public. You have no remorse for the crimes you have committed, and repeatedly smiled and giggled throughout the court proceedings, which is rude and very telling of your personality. You will receive 4 years and a £90 fine for the possession of Class A drugs, 5 years for assault, 15 years for rape, 10 years for conspiring abduction and false imprisonment, 14 years for human trafficking, and life for the murder of Scot Guilds. You will receive a minimum of 78 years imprisonment with no chance of parole. Take him down!"

Jason's smug smile dropped from his face, and he began to yell and throw punches at the security guards. "Get the fuck off me! Get your fucking hands off me!" Another two guards ran in and finally, at 5 guards, they managed to drag him out of the courtroom.

Martha let go of Nick's hand and sighed with relief, rubbing her sweaty palms against her trousers. "We did it! We really did it!"

"We did! And Jason has yet to go to court for covering up the rape of Nadia, and we're still waiting to see if the other girls will come forward. I think with this verdict we have a very strong chance of winning that case, too. He will never see the light of day again. Even the rest of his gang are facing at least 5 years in prison for rape."

"Do you know what happened to Kevin?"

"Yeah, he got 6 months for stalking and harassment, 1 year for possession of drugs and a £90 fine, to run concurrently. He'll probably be out in 3 months, but we'll be keeping a closer eye on him now we know his history."

The detectives shared a smile of relief, not too long before leaving the courtroom. The case was finally closed, and they could finally move on knowing that Lisa Marsh received the justice she so deserved.

Printed in Great Britain
by Amazon

85932290R00109